I0587081

Shielding Bank

Charon MC
Book 15

KHLOE WREN

Books by Khloe Wren

Charon MC:
Inking Eagle
Fighting Mac
Chasing Taz
Claiming Tiny
Chasing Scout
Tripping Nitro
Scout's Legacy
Mac's Destiny
Losing Bash
Finding Needles
Forging Blade
Taming Keys
Breaking Arrow
Taz's Guards
Shielding Bank

RBMC: SA:
Spark's rising
Croc's Pledge

Fire and Snow:
Guardian's Heart
Noble Guardian
Guardian's Shadow
Fierce Guardian
Necessary Alpha
Protective Instincts

Other Titles:
Fireworks
Scarred Perfection
Scandals: Zeck
FireStarter
Deception
Mine To Bear
The Warrior, The Witch
And The Wombat
Insatiable Ghost Monster

ISBN: 978-0-6451747-8-6
Copyright © Khloe Wren 2022

Cover Credits:
Model: Kevin Davis and Ryan McNulty
Photographer: Golden Czermak of FuriousFotog
Digital Artist: Khloe Wren
Editing Credits:
Editor: Carolyn Depew of Write Right

Acknowledgements

I feel like I start each of these the same way, but my wonderful husband and daughters really are the biggest support to me and enable me to write every single one of my books.

I hit burnout at the end of 2018, then Covid hit and things got worse for my mental health/writing. It's been damn hard, and many, many release plans had to be changed. I'm hopefully out the other side now so am looking forward to writing up a storm in the near future.

Bank's book was one of those stories I had to put off. I've had his story in my mind for over a year now and I'm so glad to have finally gotten his story told. It includes elements of my own past which mean this book will always be special to me, not only because it is my first MM romance.

On that note, a huge thanks to Golden Czermak. Not only for the amazing cover image but also for answering all my (no doubt) annoying questions as I wrote this and for reading over it in the end to check I'd done things right. Also thanks to Eden Bradley for her help in answering other queries in regards to this unique couple!

To Stacey and Jo-Carol for your help with all things Texan… and skunk related. I love that with your help, I can put some quirky Texan things in my stories. (And I almost, sorta want a pet skunk now.)

To Kevin Davis and Ryan McNulty, your chemistry is off the charts and you are both perfect for Bomber and Bank. Thank you for being brave enough to do this shoot with Golden, and for allowing me the honor of purchasing an image from it to use on this book.

To Christine Feehan, our week together where we both wrote up a storm was just what I needed to get back on track. And Renee, thank you so much for your help with the Spanish (Mexican) translations.

To Ann Jensen, being able to cross our worlds over and work together was such a pleasure and I can't wait to see where we both go with future projects.

To Janine Bosco, it's thanks to your innovative anthologies that you run with your TNTNYC event, that I got to work with Ann in the first place.

To my editor, Carolyn, as always thank you for all your hard work. This one wasn't even down to the wire! And to Kelly and Erin for proofreading over it.

To Fiona, so many fictional trees were grown to get this book written. Also to Chris, our week of writing flat out hidden away at your mountain home got this thing done in the end. I couldn't have done it without you both.

Lastly, to you who's reading this. Thank you so much for taking a chance with me and I hope you enjoy reading Shielding Bank as much as I did writing it.

xo

Khloe Wren

Biography

Khloe Wren lives in rural South Australia with her husband, two daughters and an ever changing list of animals!

She started writing in 2013 and has published over 40 books since then in the romantic suspense genre. She writes both paranormal and contemporary stories, including her best selling series Charon MC.

Khloe enjoys writing outside of the box and she loves her heroes strong, and her heroines even stronger.

Charon:

Char·on \ˈsher-ən, ˈker-ən, -än\

In Greek mythology, the Charon is the ferryman who takes the dead across either the river Styx or Acheron, depending on whether the soul's destination is the Elysian Fields or Hades.

Chapter 1

Sunday 15th September 2019
Bank

After installing the last of the side shelves on Bomber's brand-new barbeque, I stood and took a step back, running my gaze over the whole thing to make sure I hadn't missed anything obvious.

Scout clapped me on the back. "Looking good, brother."

The Charons' president's praise made me uncomfortable, since I didn't feel like I deserved it. Anyone could have done what I just did. "You bought the thing, I just put it together."

He chuckled. "That's the most important part. It was pretty fucking useless in the box. And seriously, I was dreading having to put the bitch together. Flat packs are not my friend."

My cheeks heated a little at the club president's words. I felt like shit for not buying anything for Bomber's housewarming. When I'd attempted to get something, my girlfriend, Karen, who was with me at the time, had made her thoughts clear on the idea. Since I hadn't wanted to deal with her losing her temper over it, here I was putting my time in instead.

"Guess now it's done, I should get going."

Scout gripped my shoulder. "You should stay and have a drink or two with us, Bank. It's Bomber's housewarming. A few of the old ladies will be here any minute with food to cook on this beast. Only logical that you stay to make sure this thing works."

I nodded. That made sense. Surely, Karen would understand that and not get in my face too much over the extra time I was spending away from home. "Yeah, okay."

"Good man. Come with me and get a beer while we wait on the food."

Pulling my phone out as we walked, I shot off a quick text to Karen before flipping my phone on silent and pocketing it. She wasn't going to be happy about me staying and I'd pay for it later but for now, I was going to enjoy a little time with my club brothers.

Karen and I had been together for a little over three years but she'd never been happy about how much time I had to give to the club. Considering I didn't actually spend all that much time with my club brothers, I wasn't sure why she got so upset the few occasions I did.

I often wondered if the club even wanted me as a brother anymore. Thanks to Karen, I basically only came to stuff that was required. Since no one had ever chased me down to ask why I wasn't at social events, I could only conclude no one fucking missed me.

I sighed as we reached the cooler and Taz handed us both a bottle.

"Here you go, mates."

I mumbled a thanks to the big Aussie as I popped the top and took a mouthful of the cool, bitter brew. Even though it was late October, today had been warm and the cold liquid felt damn good going down. Good enough, I moaned as I took my second swig.

When the hairs on the back of my neck tingled, I looked

around to see who was focused on me. My gaze clashed with Bomber's and the heat in his eyes froze me to the spot as memories flashed in my mind of what had happened the last time he looked at me like that. It'd been six and a half years ago, the last time Bomber was home.

"Getcha ass over here, boy."

Bomber was twenty-four years older than me. The age gap should probably bother me, but it didn't. The man was hot. Square jaw covered in scruff he'd have to shave off before he went back on deployment, green eyes that could look right inside a man. That gaze had seen too much. Seen things I'd tried to hide. MCs weren't exactly known as a safe place for same-sex couples.

I wasn't gay, but rather bisexual. I made use of the club whores the same as the other brothers, but these past few months since Bomber had been back, I'd found my gaze following him around more and more.

"Ain't telling you again."

His voice was gravelly as hell at the best of times, but right now it was even more so. The sound sent a shiver down my spine that landed in my cock, making me instantly hard. But I didn't move. I couldn't. We were in the rear yard of the clubhouse, and it was well past dark. I was back in the shadows and had hoped they'd keep me hidden as I watched Bomber, but he'd seen me and now he was calling me out.

With a growl and his head lowered, he prowled over to me. Out of reflex, I stepped back but the fence stopped my retreat. Next thing I knew, Bomber's right hand was wrapped around the front of my throat while his left palm slapped against the fence near my shoulder. Swallowing the best I could against his grip, I trembled as arousal and fear mixed together into a storm within me.

"Seen how you watch me, boy. Seen how you've tried to make me fucking jealous with the whores. You ready to own up to your feelings yet?"

His scent surrounded me, making my cock throb. Motor oil and leather, with just a hint of whatever soap he'd used. My brain muddled, making speech near impossible. I licked my lips to wet them, and his gaze zeroed in on it.

He tightened his grip for a few moments before loosening it. "Say. It."

I was so on edge that my voice was little more than a whisper. "Kiss me."

"Close enough." His grumbled words sent another jolt of heat through me that had me slapping my hands against the rough timber of the fence to stop myself from grabbing his hips. I didn't want to do anything to risk ending whatever was happening between us.

With a low growl, he shifted his grip up my throat until he forced my face into the angle he wanted, then he leaned in. The moment he pressed his firm lips against mine, I gasped in pleasure as my cock throbbed behind my fly. Making the most of my mouth opening, he slid his tongue in and stroked it against mine. Unable to keep my hands off him now, I gripped his hips and tried to tug his body in against me, but he held himself away, not allowing me to move him. A whimper tore from my throat but before I could get up in my head about the rejection, his left hand was between us, flicking open the button on my jeans and lowering the zipper.

My breath caught in my throat when he clamped his teeth down on my lower lip a moment before he released me while he shoved his hand into my pants, under my boxer-briefs to wrap his fingers around my throbbing cock.

"Fuck!"

A full body shudder shook me while he smirked and ran his thumb over the head of my dick before proceeding to stroke me from root to tip, the whole while his hand on my throat kept me locked against the fence. I was helpless to whatever Bomber wanted to do to me, and it was the hottest fucking encounter I'd ever had.

"You want me to make you come, you gotta earn that. On your knees, boy."

Suddenly his hands were off me and he stepped away, the cold air of the night flowing between us clearing my head enough that I could hear the party going on around us. Inhaling deeply as Bomber went for his own belt and fly, my gaze caught on the action behind him. The sight of the club whores who were being used by brothers the way Bomber wanted to use me washed over me like a bucket of ice water.

I shook my head. I couldn't do this. Couldn't let the club see that I liked men as well as women. Couldn't have Bomber treat me as nothing more than a male club whore. Tears stung my eyes, making me feel even smaller, more ashamed. Shoving my now soft cock away and zipping up my pants, I didn't bother with the button before I dashed to the side and sprinted for the back door of the clubhouse before shit could escalate more than it already had.

Fuck this night.

"Food is here! Bank, getcha ass over here and let's fire up this grill you built."

Scout's shout pulled me from my trip down memory lane and with a wince, I forced my gaze away from Bomber, who was still staring back at me. Draining the rest of my beer, I grabbed a fresh one before I went over to join the club president.

Bomber

Clenching my jaw in frustration as Bank ran from me again, I went over to the cooler to get myself a fresh beer.

"Hey, mate. Here you go."

"Thanks."

Taz was one of several new faces around the Charon MC that hadn't been here six and a bit years ago when I was last home. He was also one of my new neighbors. As far as I could tell, I was the seventh Charon MC brother to move into a house on this street. Scout was talking about petitioning the township council to change the street name. To be honest, I wasn't sure if he was joking or not.

"Looking like we're gonna lose that man soon if something doesn't change."

I turned back to the big Aussie. "You talking about Bank?"

He nodded. "Yeah, mate. He's been coming to fewer events over the last year, but he's really been avoiding shit these last couple months. He's always at church and the mandatory stuff, but this little get-together is the first social thing I've seen him at in a bloody long time."

Lifting my beer, I took a long pull before I responded. I didn't want to say something that would hint at what had happened between us all those years ago. Nothing spread faster in an MC than gossip. If I gave away that I felt more for Bank than any of my other club brothers, it'd be all over the club before the sun set. And since no one seemed to realize Bank liked both men and women, I didn't think he would appreciate me outing him. "You got any idea why?"

"Pretty sure it's mostly due to that bitch of his. Karen rides his ass hard. Every time she comes around to a club function, they always end up arguing. Not sure why he's keeping her 'round. He never patched her, so he can't be serious about her."

Taz shrugged and moved away toward his wife, who'd just come into the yard. He grabbed hold of his one-year-old daughter to swing her up into the air, making the little girl squeal with happiness.

Tearing my gaze from the sight that had caused an ache in my heart, I faced the small gathering of brothers and old ladies around my new grill that Bank had built for me. Seeing all the happy couples, along with that look we'd just shared, I was seriously wondering if it wasn't too late to see if something would work between us, assuming he'd get rid of that viper of his sometime soon. Taz's words about how Bank had changed since I'd been home had a spark of hope igniting deep in my soul.

As a gay man in the Air Force, it wasn't like I'd had a heap of opportunities to date or even hook up. Pretty sure most of my section had assumed I was celibate because I never took up the freely offered pussy. If any of them had guessed I was gay, they'd never said anything to me. Although, that might have been because as the squadron's mechanic, they wanted to be on my good side.

Here in the Charons, I'd never hidden my sexuality. Didn't have to. My club brothers accepted me just as I was, but still, I didn't go around flaunting it. It had been a damn long time since I'd had any sort of serious relationship. Although, not to say I hadn't had the occasional hook up, because I wasn't actually celibate. I'd just always kept them away from both my military and club brothers.

Except that night six and a half years ago when I'd nearly

gotten Bank on his knees in the rear yard of the clubhouse. Closing my eyes as my cock started to harden, I mentally shook away the memories. Last thing I needed was everyone currently in my yard to see me hard as concrete. Rumors would surely fly over who had me worked up.

Opening my eyes, I lifted my beer and drained the bottle in a couple of gulps. The cold liquid sliding down my throat soothed some of my nerves and allowed me to focus on walking over to the grill. "Got it working?"

"Like a dream. Bank does solid work. Always has." Scout had his son on his hip. Joey wasn't quite one, and he clung to his dad as he watched the older kids running around my yard. I was still wrapping my head around the fact that our prez had kids. Fuck. We were the same age and now he had a six-year-old daughter and an infant son. While I was still alone. Fuck.

Marie, Scout's old lady, was fussing around Bank, making him put on an apron before she handed him some tongs and a container full of sausages and burger patties. I hoped like hell there were some steaks in there too.

Bulldog, one of the older brothers, slapped me on the shoulder. He'd been the VP when I was home, but he'd recently retired from the role. Poor bastard had arthritis in his hips that made it difficult for him to ride, so he'd stepped aside for Mac, one of the younger guys, to move into the VP role.

"How you settling in so far, Bomber?"

Nodding, I turned my attention to my friend. "It's going well. Working down at the shop with Scout. Bikes are a hell of a lot simpler than the shit I was working on overseas."

Bulldog laughed. "I bet." He grew serious. "Having a solid job you enjoy is a good thing, but what about outside of that?" He flicked his gaze over to Bank before returning it to me. "You two spoken much since you got back?"

Clenching my jaw, I took in Bulldog. "You saw what happened six years ago between us, didn't you?"

He gave me a slow nod. "Yeah, you were both pretty wasted that night. Wasn't sure either of you would even fucking remember, but then you were deployed and didn't bother to come home again between your stints overseas. And he went and hooked up with that viper of his."

Fuck, I needed another drink for this conversation.

"You want a beer?"

"Yeah, grab me one."

I went over to the cooler that was now unmanned, since Taz was busy with his family. After grabbing a couple bottles, I walked back to Bulldog, who had moved further to the side of my yard, away from the others who were hanging around. After handing him one, I opened mine and took a long drink before I spoke.

"I haven't had a chance to talk to Bank yet. He's a hard man to get alone, and I'm not sure what the point would be in trying so long as he's with Karen."

Bulldog shook his head. "That boy ain't planning to settle down with her forever. He'd have put his patch on her back long before now if he was serious. Karen's the only long-term girlfriend in the club who isn't an old lady... which I'm fucking thankful for. No way do I ever want to have to protect that piece of trash. We're all waiting for the day Bank finally shoves her to the curb and we don't have to put up with her shit anymore." He paused to take a drink. "I think he's only staying with her in an attempt to fit in with the club."

Before I could respond, my back door banged open and the woman in question came barreling out, bringing all the drama in the world with her. Turning my attention to Bank as she stormed over to him, I crossed my arms and waited for the fireworks. Bank had stilled, his eyes open wide like prey when a predator came at it, as she approached. Her voice was quiet enough I couldn't make out the words, but the way Bank shrunk into himself and shook his head made it clear she wasn't saying anything nice to the man. My free hand clenched into a fist when she lifted her hand and poked him hard in the chest, hard enough to rock him.

Bank had always been pretty submissive in nature, a people-pleaser who always put himself last. He'd struggle to break up with anyone, no matter how much he needed to, but I'd find a way to help him. Even if he never gave me the time of day again, I'd get him free from the harpy who was currently railing at him for not being home at her beck and call.

"I won't let him avoid me for much longer."

Bulldog nodded. "The sooner, the better. She'll have him quitting the club before long, then he'll have no protection from her."

I turned back to look at Bulldog with a frown, "What do you mean protection? You think she's doing more than what she's doing now?"

Bulldog suddenly looked about ten years older. "He hides it well, but I've seen enough abuse victims to know what's going on. I'd put money on you finding bruises if you get him without a shirt. But that's something else he hasn't done in years. Most of the younger guys end up wearing their cut with no shirt in the summer. Not Bank. It can be hot as hell and he'll still be wearing at least a t-shirt, if not a long sleeve shirt."

The thought of Bank being physically abused was enough to have me taking a step toward him but before I made it more than a few feet, chaos ran into my yard. Ariel and Ashlynn were both six years old, lived next door to each other and were nothing but trouble. The whole club even called them Double

Trouble whenever they were together.

Ashlynn's voice was loud enough to silence the yard and draw every eye to her, "Daddy! Look what we found!"

"Where the hell did you two find fucking skunks?"

Needles did not sound happy with his daughter and suddenly I wasn't so upset at the fact I didn't have kids yet.

Chapter 2

Ten minutes earlier
Ariel

"They're so cute!"

I looked around to see if the little babies' momma was near but couldn't find anything.

My best friend, Ashlynn, moved toward them. "We can't leave them here alone! They'll die."

Nodding, I followed her and scooped up one of the cute little black and white furry babies. I wasn't entirely sure what they were. Kittens, maybe? Once I had it in my hands and got a closer look, I wasn't so sure.

"What do you think they are, Ash?"

"Duh, they're skunks. I read this blog post about them. You can totally keep them as pets. And they don't squirt stinky stuff when they're this little."

Excitement sped through me. "Really? They're so cute! I want to keep them. And there's two! We can have one each. Let's go show the others."

Everyone was over at Uncle Bomber's house, which was next door to my house. There was a creek that ran behind all the houses, so Ash and I had gone exploring when the adults got boring.

We both turned and ran for Uncle Bomber's yard, Ashlynn in the lead because her legs were longer.

"Daddy! Look what we found!"

I skidded to a stop behind Ashlynn, staring wide-eyed as both our dads came toward us not looking happy.

"Where the hell did you two find fucking skunks?"

Oh, no, Ash's dad was swearing. That wasn't good. Especially since her mom didn't tell him off for it either. Maybe this wasn't such a great idea after all.

I lifted my little skunk up and rubbed my cheek over its soft fur.

"Ariel, explain yourself right now."

I looked up at Scout, my adopted dad. "We found them, Papa. They have no momma, so we saved them."

The way he sighed and rubbed a hand over his face didn't fill me with confidence.

"Kiddo, I'm sure their momma was just off hunting for food or somethin'. She'll come back and find her kits missing. You need to go put them back right now. We'll go with you."

"Aw, shit. Incoming!"

I wasn't sure who'd called out, but I glanced around my dad to see a much bigger skunk running through the yard.

"Oh, no."

Dad growled, "Damn straight. Put those babies down and move away from them, right now."

Whenever Papa got that tone of voice, I did exactly what he said. Ash and I set the babies on the grass next to each other, then turned to run toward the women. Mommy didn't look any happier than Papa had, but she held her arms out and I ran into them.

"Girls, you have got to stop trying to gather wild animals for pets."

I turned my head to look back toward the skunks. Everyone had cleared that side of the yard and the momma had gone over to her babies and was sniffing them, nosing them around. My eyes stung and I sniffled. I'd really wanted to keep that little baby skunk.

"Men are so fucking useless."

I gasped at the angry woman who stormed over toward the animals.

"Karen, what the hell are you doing?" Uncle Bank tore off his apron and tossed the tongs aside before he came after Karen. But he was too late. She pulled out a gun and without any hesitation aimed it at the animals. I screamed for her to stop, Ash joining me. I didn't want any of them to die! We'd been trying to save the babies!

Mommy tightened her grip on me when I tried to pull free, Bess was next to me holding Ash back too, but we both kept screaming, hoping one of the adults would do something.

The gun went off with a loud bang that made my ears ring. Mommy's hand went to my eyes, covering them but before she did, I caught sight of one of the babies jerking. That mean woman had shot one of the babies! A sob tore from me, and I turned in against Mommy, burying my face against her tummy as I continued to cry.

Bomber

What a fucking nightmare.

Karen was something else. All she had to do was stand back with everyone else and that momma skunk would have gathered her babies and left peacefully. But, no, the stupid bitch came out guns blazing. I wasn't sure if she'd actually aimed at the kits but that's what she hit, killing one of the babies with her first bullet. Before she got off the second shot, the momma skunk went for her, turning around to spray her just as she pulled the trigger again.

Talk about chaos. I was standing back with Bulldog and a few others, basically in shock. In the course of about five minutes, my yard had turned into a fucking circus. Now Karen was screaming because she was covered in skunk stink, Ashlynn and Ariel were crying their hearts out, and Scout, who'd handed off his son to one of the other old ladies since Marie had her hands full with Ariel, along with Needles, had grabbed plastic bags to deal with the dead skunks.

I might be a mechanic by trade, but I'd always had a strong affinity with animals. As a kid, I'd had all sorts of random beasties as pets. Well, not really pets. I'd rescue wildlife, nurse them back to health and release them. So, I followed Needles and Scout, scooping up the remaining baby skunk while the other two dealt with the dead animals. Karen had managed to kill both the momma and one of the kits. Fucking bitch. I glared over to where she was, railing at Bank like it was his fucking fault she was a lunatic. A lunatic with a fucking gun. Just what we needed.

Zara, Mac's old lady, headed over toward them and after a couple minutes, the three of them headed around the side of my house. I hoped she stunk like skunk for a fucking week.

Scout handed his bag over to Needles to deal with before he came over to me shaking his head.

"What the hell we gonna do with that little thing? Why isn't it spraying like its momma did?"

I ran a finger down the kit's back, soothing the animal who was shaking and clearly in distress. "They don't spray like an adult skunk until they're around three months old. It'll be fine till then. And if you did want to let Ariel keep it, you can get their scent glands removed."

He winced. "Marie will not be happy about that one. Fuck! Guess I'll be back on the damn couch because I can't let her not take responsibility for this shit. As much as Karen was the bitch who shot them, if the girls had left the animals alone in the first place, we wouldn't have a damn orphaned skunk on our hands."

Needles came up to us. "Bess will not allow a skunk anywhere near our place. Not after the damn raccoon incident last year."

I was pretty sure I didn't want to know the story behind that one. I could only imagine how Double Trouble had acquired a raccoon.

"I used to rehab wildlife when I was a kid. If you want, I can keep it here and your two little troublemakers can come over to help me care for it."

Relief washed over both men as they blew out breaths. "That'd be perfect, brother. Saved both our asses, and our daughters. Let's go tell the girls about their new responsibilities. Oh, and they'll be giving you some of their allowances to help pay for its care too."

With a nod, I followed them over to the crying girls. I liked how Scout was thinking. It was important to teach kids about consequences of poorly thought-out choices. I was more than happy to help them learn what they'd need to know to be responsible adults later in life.

As we got closer, Marie and Bess encouraged the girls to turn to face their fathers. Both had red faces and the saddest expressions I'd ever seen. I'd be a terrible girl dad. All she'd need was to flash that look at me and she'd get away with just about anything.

Scout took a deep breath before he lowered down to kneel in front of the two girls.

"I know you both only wanted to save those two little baby kits, but you can't take wild animals from their nests like that. Just because they're alone when you find them, doesn't mean they're orphans. Animals often leave their babies alone for short periods of time while they go find food." He shifted his gaze between the two girls, who were still sniffling but were trying to stop their tears in the face of Scout's lecture.

"Now we have an orphan skunk that needs to be cared for."

Both Bess and Marie started to shake their heads but before they said a word, Scout held up a palm. "Stop, ladies. This isn't going where you're thinkin'." Then he focused back on the girls. "Neither of you are getting to keep that little kit. Your Uncle Bomber has offered to take care of it. He's looked after orphaned wild animals before, so he knows what to do. But you two are going to help him. Your allowances will be docked to pay for its necessities, and after school you're both going to be visiting Uncle Bomber's house to help him take care of it. Because as much as neither of you pulled the trigger, it was your decision to take those babies from their nest that started everything that happened afterward. And that means you both need to help deal with the fallout. Understood?"

"Yes, Papa."

"Yes, Uncle Scout."

Both girls still appeared miserable, but they looked to me with a little hope in their gazes.

Yep, I could never have daughters. I wouldn't survive.

Then Ariel frowned back toward her father with a glint in her gaze that spelled trouble for Scout. "What about the mean lady? What punishment does Karen get?"

"Don't you worry about her, Ariel. The momma skunk got her good. She's gonna stink to high heaven for a while."

The girl nodded. "Good. I hope she stinks for a month."

That had all of us chuckling, and the air seemed to clear of the tension that settled over my yard after Karen had decided to kill a couple innocent animals.

I held out the little kit to Ariel, "Here you go. I need you two to take care of it while I go sort out a box and find some food for it to munch on."

As I walked inside, I couldn't help but wonder what sort of shit storm Bank was dealing with. She was not going to react well to being sprayed. I suspect she'd respond equally badly to the long process of getting rid of the stink.

Chapter 3

Bank

Karen raged the entire way around to the front of the house. The stench was bad enough to make my fucking eyes water. I was glad Zara had stepped up and offered to help us deal with the stink. She and Mac lived just up the road from Bomber's place so we could easily walk there.

Staying beside Zara, I slowed my pace, allowing Karen to get a distance in front of us. Between her rage and the smell, I was happy to let her storm ahead.

"She always this, um, intense?"

I nodded. "Pretty much. You have enough tomato juice to do this?"

She shook her head with a smirk. "Old wives' tale, that one. I mean, if you want, we can start with that. It'd be fun to watch her look like an extra from a slasher movie, especially after she killed those poor skunks like she did. But it won't help with the smell."

"What are you going to do then?"

I'd never been stupid enough to get sprayed by a skunk myself, so I had no clue about any of this shit.

"Hydrogen peroxide, baking soda and a little soap. It'll take a couple washes, but she'll be fine. We have an outdoor shower at our place that'll work perfectly." She looked at me with a sly smile. "Unless you want to hose her off. I can totally forget to mention the shower."

I chuckled but shook my head. "I do not want to see how bad she'd lose her temper if I had to hose her off."

She shrugged as we caught up to Karen, who was impatiently waiting on the sidewalk in front of Zara's place.

"You two done flirting?"

I'd been relaxing, chatting with Zara, enjoying her calm and humor, but in seconds it all evaporated under Karen's bullshit. Usually, I didn't try to defend myself with her, especially in front of others, but her utter disrespect of Zara, who had left the barbecue to help us out, had me snapping back before I could think better of it.

"For fuck's sake, Karen, cut the crap for once. Zara was just telling me they have an outdoor shower you can use so you don't have to get hosed down with cold water. Great way to thank the woman."

The withering look she gave me told me that I was just making shit worse for later and with a shake of my head, we followed Zara around the side of their house to the backyard.

"Here you go. We installed it a few months back. Kids get so damn grubby. It's easier to rinse them off out here rather than have them drag sand and mud all through the house. Same goes for the men when they're covered in grease and dirt. I'll mix up the peroxide solution and be out with it in a few minutes, along with a bag for your clothes and something for you to wear home."

When Karen remained silent, I gave Zara a smile. "Thanks, Zara."

As soon as she headed inside, Karen started in on me, "You can stop watching her ass, you know."

I sighed. "Karen, I ain't even looking in her direction. Enough with the jealousy. I've never once stepped out on you, and you know it."

Damn woman went through my phone often enough, she'd know if I had a side piece. And with all the grief I copped from her, like I'd sign myself up for another dose of that shit from a second lover.

An image of Bomber standing over me filled my mind. Would he be as demanding as Karen? Expect me to grovel and pander to his every need?

Suddenly, I couldn't stay here. Couldn't stay still or take another word out of Karen's mouth.

"I'm gonna go get your car and bring it up here for after you get done. Be nice to Zara, or you'll have Mac to answer to."

I didn't give her time to respond, just took off back around the side of the house. My phone vibrated in my pocket as I hit the sidewalk and I pulled it out to see who was messaging. My steps faltered when Bomber's name came up as though he'd heard my thoughts or something.

"You need me, call. No matter what, I got you."

An ache started in my chest. Was he for real? I'd figured with how I ran off all those years ago, followed by him not coming home between deployments, he'd decided I wasn't worth the effort. I'd never admit it to anyone, but ever since that night, he'd been front and center in nearly every erotic dream I had. My subconscious liked to play out that night to a very different conclusion. One where I didn't run but instead dropped to my knees and wrapped my mouth around his cock. Followed by him dragging me upstairs to his room, where we'd spend all night together.

With a huff, I deleted the message, making sure all traces were gone from my phone. Last thing I needed was Karen seeing it. Then I went to get her car. I'd have to drive her home, but I knew my bike would be fine out in front of Bomber's place until I could come back and get it. With how many Charon brothers that now lived on this street, it was about as safe as the clubhouse these days.

Unfortunately, it didn't take nearly long enough for me to fetch the car or for Karen to finish washing off. Before I was ready to endure more, we were alone in her car as I drove us home.

"You going to apologize?"

I bit down the sigh as I hit the signal and turned down the next street.

"What, exactly, do you think I need to be sorry about?"

She huffed and slapped at my shoulder, hard enough to leave a sting in her wake.

"If you hadn't stayed longer than you were supposed to, I wouldn't have had to come looking for you. None of this would have happened if you'd just come home on time."

I took a deep breath before slowly letting it out.

"Karen, you know I'm a brother in the club, I can't run out on everything all the time. Scout — you know, the president — asked me to stay to make sure the grill was working. I can't turn down a request from Scout."

She huffed again. "Sure, you can. Not like they want you around anyway. Since you never did any military time, they're all just tolerating you. You really need to wake up and see that and move on. There are better things you could fill your days with."

I clenched my jaw at the familiar taunt she threw at me. I wasn't the only Charon brother who'd not gone into the service, but we were the minority.

"Whatever, babe."

This time she planted her fist against my bicep in the same spot she'd slapped, and the arm deadened instantly. "Don't you dare *whatever* me! I'm trying to help you! You'd be so much better off without them all holding you down. They're constantly making demands on you, wanting your time and what do you get for it? They never do a damn thing for us!"

She kept up her yelling and ranting the whole way back home. She managed to quiet down some while she moved between the car and house, but the moment that front door was shut, she turned on me and I knew I was in for a long, fucking night.

Bank

After waking alone, I rolled over with a groan and sat on the side of the mattress before I forced myself to my feet. Pain shot through my body as I stumbled into the bathroom. Since I was naked, I couldn't hide from what the mirror told me.

I was fucking pathetic. What kind of man lets a woman beat on him? I flexed my right bicep, wincing at the pain that radiated from the cut I'd gotten last night after Karen had thrown her glass. It hit the wall next to me and shattered, the shards cutting into my arm. Naturally, the same arm she'd already bruised on the car ride earlier.

That cut wasn't my only injury. My left shoulder was screaming at me from when she'd grabbed my wrist and wrestled my arm up behind my back. I also had bruising on my wrist from her tight grip. There were angry, red lines across my chest where she'd scratched her nails into me deeply, and a large bruise on my thigh that was healing from when she'd lost her temper earlier in the week. My head ached, and my scalp was tender from her yanking my hair. With a shake of my head, I turned from the mirror, unable to look myself in the eye, and caught sight of my knuckles. They were undamaged because I couldn't bring myself to raise a hand to a woman, even when she was raising hers to me.

Flipping on the shower, I got in, not even bothering with hot water. I didn't deserve the comfort the heat would bring.

As the pain throbbed through my body, my thoughts spiraled, backed up by her words. All the times she told me how useless I was, how pathetic I was to still be hanging around a club that obviously didn't want me. How I was lucky that she continued to attempt to look out for me, care for me, when no one else would.

After quickly washing myself, I turned off the shower and dried with rough strokes of the towel before wrapping it around my waist. I rubbed some antibacterial shit into the scratches but didn't bother covering them with bandages. None were bleeding and they'd heal faster open to the air. Grabbing the shaving cream, I lathered up and made fast work of getting rid of the stubble that Karen hated the feel of against her skin.

The door banged open and on reflex, I jerked, leaving a cut on my jaw line with my razor as I did.

"Fuck."

Reaching over to grab a handful of tissues from the box, I pressed them to the cut.

"Oh, Bank! What did you do to yourself? Here let me take a look."

I ran my gaze over her, not trusting how nice she was being but unwilling to risk her getting angry. I let her take over control of the tissues as she dealt with the small cut that I knew wouldn't bleed for much longer. She took the razor and gently finished off shaving my face while she held the tissues firmly with her other hand.

This was her cycle. She'd lose her temper, lash out, then afterward, she'd be all soft and loving to me. An unspoken apology for the earlier roughness. Somewhere deep down, I knew it was a fucked-up cycle, but I couldn't seem to find the courage to break things off with her.

I really was the worthless piece of shit she called me. Couldn't even leave a woman who treated me like garbage half the time, because when she wasn't laying into me, she was good to me. She was the only one who'd never left me.

My mom had been young, still in high school, when she'd gotten pregnant. Her folks hadn't allowed her to terminate the pregnancy, even though it was the result of rape. Instead, they'd waited for my birth, then when my mother couldn't stand the sight of me, my grandparents shipped me off to Bridgewater to live with my Uncle Samuel.

He'd been in his fifties when he'd taken me in. Never married, we were all each other had. Uncle Samuel had been old-school and his love had been gruff, but it had been there. He'd raised me to respect those around me, never raise a hand to a woman, to work hard and always pay my dues.

But he'd died of a heart attack four years ago. I'd met Karen six months later. I'd been struggling to deal with my grief when she came around and made me feel like a million bucks with all her compliments and attention.

Karen's voice, all sweetness this morning, cut into my thoughts. "I think we should take a trip. A romantic getaway for a few days. We've both been so stressed lately, it'll be good for us to travel and relax. What do you think? We could head out this morning."

This was different. She'd never once suggested we go away. "I'll need to check with work. Not sure I can get the time off on such short notice."

My heart rate kicked up when her gaze narrowed. Since she was still holding the sharp razor near my face and I knew how fast her mood could change, I was quick to continue, "But I agree. A few days away would be nice. Let me make some calls and see what I can sort out."

It might end up costing me my damn job, but I couldn't handle her getting violent with me again. Not when I was still so damn sore from last night. Not when she had a fucking blade near my face that I knew from experience she'd use on me if she lost her temper again.

"While you do that, I'm going to run down to the store to grab some stuff. We can head off when I get back."

Grabbing a towel, she wiped her hands before she turned and left me to wash off my face and finish dealing with the cut, all the while I tried to think of what I could say to my boss about this last-minute leave I needed that wouldn't cost me my fucking job.

He already didn't like that I was in an MC and needed time off for runs. But since the MC didn't own a landscaping business, I couldn't really work for the club.

One more thing that proved Karen had a point with how much I didn't fit in with the Charons. Maybe getting away for a few days to clear my head wasn't such a bad idea after all.

Chapter 4

Bank

In the two hours it took Karen to return from wherever the fuck she'd gone, I'd managed to call in enough favors from my work buddies that I had my jobs covered for the next three days. The boss wasn't happy but so far, I wasn't fired, so I was counting it as a win.

I had my bag packed and was tidying up the kitchen when she came home, already talking before she was through the door. "You ready to go, babe?"

Putting away the last mug, I turned her way. "Yeah, where we heading?"

She grabbed my bag off the floor and grinned at me, looking as relaxed and happy as she had when we'd first gotten together.

"I found the most gorgeous little hotel up in Philly. It's going to be great!"

I winced, "Babe, I only got three days off work. Unless we're flying, not sure this is going to work."

Her expression darkened and I waited for the explosion. Her temper was on a hair trigger these days, but she couldn't honestly expect me to agree to spending the three days in a fucking cage to have what? One night at whatever hotel she'd found. Even if we took turns driving and didn't stop to sleep overnight somewhere, it'd probably take a little over twenty-four hours to get there, and that again to get back. She hadn't thought this through. It wouldn't work.

"We're not flying, the road trip is the best part of getting away." She huffed. "You always do this. Try to ruin my plans for you before we get to enjoy them. I won't let you this time. Let's go." She turned around. "Oh... and take that thing off. This trip has nothing to do with that club."

I gritted my teeth. I felt naked when I wasn't wearing my club colors. "I'll take it off when we cross out of Texas."

She huffed again, but knew it was the best she was going to get out of me. After locking up, I followed her to the car, where she put my bag in the trunk for me, which was odd. Normally, she made me do any lifting or carrying. Clearly, she wasn't going to budge about the road trip, and I really didn't want to be stuck in a cage with her in a shit of a mood, so I plastered a grin on my face and got in.

Maybe I could fly back earlier, let her drive herself back when she was ready.

By the time Bridgewater was in the rear-view mirror, Karen had headphones on and was fast asleep. With a shake of my head, I flipped the radio on to an old-school rock station and kept the volume low enough Karen wouldn't hear it if she woke.

So much for the road trip being the best part.

By the time we rolled into Philly late the next evening, I was back behind the wheel and about ready to explode. We'd only stopped for a few hours overnight. Karen had insisted we needed to get to Philly today. I was fucking tired, sick of driving, and over being stuck in a damn cage. Not that being on my bike would have been any better on this length of a trip.

When she directed me to pull up at the Five Point Hotel, I shook my head, but honestly was too fucking tired to argue with her. This place looked like every other middle-of-the-road hotel I'd ever seen. Tomorrow, after I'd gotten some sleep, I was gonna ask some questions. I didn't care if she lost her fucking temper, I was done with this whole getaway already.

Once I was parked, I stayed silent as I got out and went around to the trunk. But she beat me there, handing me my bag and grabbing hers before closing the lid. What the fuck was going on with her?

I rubbed my eyes with my free hand, trying to get my brain to clear.

"Oh, my poor baby. So tired. Let's go check in and get up to our room. Then I'll have a quick shower before I make you feel all better."

The purr in her voice had my cock twitching in anticipation. Didn't seem to matter how tired my brain was, my dick was always up for some action. Especially since it had been a while since I'd gotten any. First thing Karen did whenever she got upset was refuse me any kind of intimacy or sex. And lately, she seemed to always be pissed off about something.

Following her through the front doors, I stayed quiet as she handled checking us in. I was about to fall asleep on my feet by the time she took my hand, and we headed toward the elevators. Neither of us said a word until we were inside our fifth-floor room. A glance around showed me it really was nothing special. We definitely didn't need to drive halfway across the damn country in order to find a place like this, that was for sure.

"Why don't you go lie down before you fall over, babe? I'm go take my shower real quick before I join you."

"Sure."

I didn't argue because I really could use a few minutes of peace to get some fucking sleep before we did anything else. Sad day when I was too tired to fuck my woman, but I wasn't used to long-haul drives with only a couple hours sleep.

Toeing off my boots, I flopped down onto the bed and was asleep before Karen shut the bathroom door.

Bank

The snick of a door opening woke me, and I opened my eyes a fraction, hoping to see Karen coming my way naked and ready to get busy. But that's not the sight that greeted me. Nope. Karen came out of the bathroom wearing boots, jeans and a sweater. Her makeup and hair were on point and my earlier suspicions came back with a rush. Now I'd had some sleep, my mind wasn't as foggy and all the shit she'd pulled so far with this trip had me faking sleep to see what she'd do next.

Keeping her gaze on me, she tiptoed over toward our luggage. After slowly picking up her handbag, she moved to the door and slipped out. The second it shut behind her, I sat on the side of the bed and pulled on my boots. Before I slid out the door to follow, I grabbed my Charon MC cut from my bag, where Karen had forced me to store it. I felt naked without it on and if Karen was pulling shit, I wanted all the protection I could get. We were a long way from Texas, but the club had friends in clubs all over the country. After pocketing my phone and the second room keycard, I slowly opened the door to see if Karen was in view. The elevator was just closing as I peeked out. Once it was all the way closed, I entered the hallway and jogged down to the stairwell entrance. Grateful we were only five floors up, I rushed down the stairs, making it down to the ground floor in no time.

Once more, I was slow and careful with the doorway, making sure Karen wasn't anywhere close before I exited into the rear of the hotel lobby. Catching a flash of the pink sweater she was wearing, I tracked her as she went into the parking lot. Silently cursing, I followed, staying in the shadows.

It had to be past midnight by now, so it wasn't difficult to stay hidden. There also weren't many others around at this hour. But if she took off in the car, I was fucked with no way to track her. Frowning, I watched as she popped the trunk and grabbed out a black duffel I'd never seen before. Guess that answered why she hadn't let me go near the trunk on this trip. But what the fuck was in it?

Closing the lid, she turned and rushed out to the street, crossing to the other side before she started walking at a brisk pace down the sidewalk. I stayed on the opposite side of the street and a little behind her, but easily kept pace, wondering what the fuck she was up to with every step. Especially when the buildings we passed grew more and more dilapidated. The graffiti increased, as did the broken and boarded-up windows. I didn't need to be a local to know this was a dangerous part of town. What the fuck was she up to?

The further we went, the easier it was to stay hidden from Karen's sight. She never once looked behind her or anywhere other than directly in front of her. I shook my head at how careless she was. Sure, she carried a piece with her, but if someone jumped her, they'd have her pinned before she'd be able to draw it.

When she walked right up to three men standing on a corner,

I slipped deeper into the shadows, entering an abandoned building though a busted out door. Once scanning the interior to make sure I was alone, I made my way further down, looking through cracks and broken windows as I went to make sure they didn't move. Once I was opposite them, I crouched down into a corner where I could see them through a small crack in the wall. I could also hear them, not clearly, but enough to catch what they were discussing.

Karen held out the bag and one of the men snatched it from her grip and dropped it to the ground, kneeling beside it to open the thing. I blew out a breath when he lifted a brick of what had to be drugs. Fuck. No wonder she'd been so fucking moody and cagey lately. Scout was going to lose his fucking mind that Karen was dealing. Thank fuck, I'd never patched her. She wasn't an old lady, so the club had no responsibility for her. After this, neither would I.

I wouldn't tolerate her dealing fucking drugs. No matter what it took, I was going to end shit between us.

"And my payment? Is it all sorted?"

One of the men not counting the drugs nodded. "It's been arranged. Get him to this location, and you'll never see him again."

That had me cocking my head as I frowned. She hadn't wanted money? She took a slip of paper from the man, then pulled her phone out.

The guy on the ground stood with the bag. "It's all here."

My phone vibrated in my pocket, and I looked down to pull it out, shocked to see it was a text from Karen.

"Stepped out to buy smokes. Got into trouble, need you now." She'd added an address that wasn't where we were.

"That fucking bitch." I mumbled the words low, so they wouldn't travel, but had to vent some of the rage that was burning inside me. She'd arranged to have me killed in payment for her running drugs. Why? Part of me wanted to march out there with my own gun drawn and aimed at her head, like she'd done to those skunks.

Remembering the critters had me thinking of Bomber. I was gonna need some help to get out of this mess. I had no idea if the club would have my back at this point, but Bomber had messaged me promising to be there. I tapped out a quick text to him.

"Need help. In Philly. Karen set me up. I'll call when I can."

As soon as it sent, I deleted it off my phone, not wanting Karen to see I was on to her in case I needed to play along for a bit before I could get free of her.

Suddenly, the night came alive with flashing lights and sirens. Tucking my phone away, I looked out the crack to see Karen and one of the men slip down an alley as the other two men were taken to the ground by cops. Fuck. I needed to get out of here.

Spinning on my heel, I headed back the way I'd come and as I slipped out of the side of the building I was grabbed and thrown up against the wall.

"You're under arrest, asshole."

Chapter 5

Bomber

With a gasp, I sat up in bed, panting from the nightmare. Fuck. I scrubbed a hand over my face as I tried to rid my mind of the images that my imagination had created from Taz telling stories last night. I was going to knock him the fuck out the next time he got started with that shit. Damn Marines always had to poke fun at us Air Force guys. Like anyone wanted to hear about how fucked it was over there.

Shaking my head with a growl, I reached for my phone, intending on playing some music to help drown out the images. But when I saw a new message had come in from Bank, I clicked on it.

"Need help. In Philly. Karen set me up. I'll call when I can."

"Aw fuck, man. I knew that woman was bad news."

It also explained why he hadn't gotten his bike from my place yet. When he hadn't come around the next morning, I rolled it into my garage so no one would see it out there and start asking questions I didn't have answers to.

Checking the time stamp, I saw it had come through a couple of hours ago. There were no missed calls, so I tried to call him back, but it went straight to voice mail.

"Fuck!"

I needed more information. The club had recently set up a new business, Athena Security. So instead of ringing Keys at two in the morning and feeling like shit for dragging the man away from his old lady, I could call whoever was on night shift over there. Flipping through my contacts, I found the number and hit dial.

"Hey, Bomber, it's damn early for you to be making a social call."

Jacie was Taz's sister, and her Aussie accent was even stronger than her brother's. I'd heard she'd been working with the Australian Federal Police with digital surveillance stuff before she'd landed here in Bridgewater.

"You got the whole club programed into your caller ID?"

She chuckled, "Something like that. What can I do for you?"

"Bank sent me a text about two hours ago saying he was up in Philly and in trouble, that Karen had set him up. He's not answering his phone so I was hoping you could work some magic and tell me where he is exactly so I can fly up there and get him."

All levity was gone from her tone when she responded, "Leave it with me. Keep your phone handy and I'll call you back when I know something."

"Don't bother, I'm gonna grab a quick shower then come to you."

"Good deal. See you soon."

Knowing Jacie wouldn't take long to dig up something, I raced through the fastest shower I'd ever taken. Once dressed, I jumped on my bike and roared down the street, heading for the Athena Security offices. Originally it had been run out of the clubhouse, but when the building next to the gym became available two months back, Scout had snapped it up and moved the business into it.

In less than five minutes I was punching in the code to the side door and entering into the fully kitted-out office. Scout had given Keys free rein to set this place up and between him and Jacie, they'd made it look like some sort of high-tech command center straight off a movie set. A few of the other club brothers worked here too, but Keys and Jacie were the top dogs of the operation.

"Whatcha got for me?"

Before Jacie could answer my question, the door behind me opened and Keys and Scout came through. Keys went straight to sit beside Jacie, where he started tapping away at the keyboard. Scout came up beside me and gripped my shoulder.

"Heard your bike tear out and knew something must have happened."

I gave him a nod but turned back to Jacie. He'd work out what was going on soon enough without me wasting time recapping.

Jacie took the hint and started talking.

"His phone is off, so I couldn't use that to find him."

Keys cut her off. "I can get around that, give me five."

She nodded his way but continued her report to me. "Using the cameras we have around town, I was able to work out when they left Bridgewater. Following traffic cameras and whatever else I could get my hands on, I managed to determine they checked into Five Points in downtown Philly at around ten o'clock last night. I got into the hotel's surveillance cameras. Just before midnight, Karen left the hotel with Bank following her. He was clearly trying to stay hidden from her."

She looked over her shoulder at me. "I really don't like that bitch."

I chuffed. "Yeah, not sure anyone, including Bank, actually likes her. Where'd they go from the hotel?"

"They walked through downtown and into Kensington. That's a real shitty part of town, so not many cameras and I lost them. But I can tell you, both Bank and Karen went into the area, then a bunch of cop cars followed about twenty minutes later. I located Karen after the cops left the area, but no sign of Bank."

Keys sat back from his computer. "Yeah, he's in lock-up. Well, his phone is, at least." He turned to face Scout. "We got any friends in Philly? I can't think of anyone, but at this time of the morning, my brain isn't exactly firing on all cylinders."

Pulling out my phone, I flipped through my contact list, trying to remember if anyone I knew lived anywhere near Philly. I paused when I came across Static's name, a member of my squadron who'd retired about the same time I had. I remembered him mentioning he was from Philly. I had no idea if he still lived there.

"I might have a contact. An old Air Force buddy. Let me text him."

As I started to type out a message, Scout moved over to stand beside Jacie. "You keep tracking that bitch. I wanna know where she is at all times. If she comes anywhere near here, I want her grabbed and locked up."

Bank

It took fucking forever before I got the chance to make a phone call. I'd never been arrested before, so had no clue how long all this processing shit was supposed to take, but it felt like it was taking too long. Although, considering how many were in the cells with me, the wait wasn't exactly surprising but it still pissed me off. My Charon MC cut had some people leaving me alone, though it also had the opposite effect on others. A couple of guys had tried to rough me up and they'd gotten a quick lesson on how despite my lean build, I had some power behind my punches. And that while I wouldn't raise a hand to a woman, I had no problem at all knocking around men. Especially ones who thought I was an easy target.

By the time I got processed and was allowed to make a call, I was tired, frustrated, and still fucking furious at Karen's betrayal. Picking up the phone handset, I didn't need to think on who to call. The only one I wanted to hear from was Bomber. Hopefully, he'd gotten my text and I wasn't waking him up.

After the first ring, he picked up.

"Who's this?"

"Hey, Bomber, it's Bank."

Before I could say another word, Bomber cut me off.

"Thank fuck. You still in lock-up?"

That left me frowning. "How'd you know where I am?"

"I tried to call you after I saw your text, but it went straight to voice mail, so I called in to Athena and got Jacie and Keys on the case."

Fuck, he probably knew more about my situation than I did.

"Yeah, I'm still in lock-up. Being charged with dealing drugs. It's bullshit. But the fact I had nothing on me apparently just means they caught me after I'd sold them. Bomber, I didn't do anything wrong. Karen was being shady as fuck, and when she snuck out after she thought I was asleep, I followed her. You gotta believe me, brother. I had no fucking clue she's been dealing. I swear."

"Bank, take a breath, man. We know. Jacie pulled up a heap of cameras to track you down, including those in the hotel. Not sure the cops will believe us, but we believe you. Listen, I got an Air Force buddy up that way, Static. He's sorting out a lawyer for you. Don't answer any more questions until you have that lawyer with you, understand? His name is Tepes and he'll be in to see you as soon as he can this morning."

"Good, because I'm being arraigned today."

The growl that came down the line had a shiver run down my spine. I couldn't quite wrap my head around the fact he cared this much. That Jacie and Keys cared enough to get up in the middle of the night to search for me.

"Keep your chin up, Bank. We'll get you through this. I've booked a 6:15 a.m. flight, so I'll be up there by mid-morning. You need anything else before I get there, you fucking call Keys or Scout."

Shame burned my throat. The whole fucking club would know how stupid I'd been within hours, if they didn't already. Would they still want me as a member after this? Scout did not tolerate drugs at all within Bridgewater. I knew I hadn't helped Karen, but if there was any doubt in Scout's or the clubs' minds, they'd shove me out the door in a heartbeat.

"Thanks, Bomber. I appreciate it. One more thing before I hang up. Get Keys to pull the text Karen sent to my phone just before I messaged you. The address she messaged me was not where she was."

Another of his growls came down the line. "I can take a guess at what you mean. Fucking bitch. We will deal with her, don't you worry. Okay, I gotta get moving. See you soon, boy."

Him finishing off with the endearment he'd said that night all those years ago had my heart skipping a beat.

"Thanks."

Ending the call, I was led back to the cells, moving straight to the back corner where I could keep an eye on all the other fuckers in here in case anyone tried to pull more shit.

While I waited, I ran over things in my mind. My girlfriend of three years wanted me dead but didn't want to do it herself. Considering all the times she'd gotten physical with me, that didn't make sense. Why did she suddenly not want to be the one to get her hands dirty?

I shook my head. Like it fucking mattered. She was dealing drugs across state lines and had taken a hit out on me in lieu of being paid by whoever she was selling to.

The longer I stood there thinking back over our relationship, the angrier I got. With my rose-colored glasses well and truly off, I suddenly saw things in a new light. Karen's behavior had been over the top for a long time, and the good times had been getting less and less to the point now where I struggled to remember the last time I even fucking smiled around her. Why the hell had I stayed with her?

That question forced me to see parts of myself I didn't want to examine. Forced me to admit that what I'd been feeling for Bomber all those years ago was more than mere infatuation. That he'd torn out my heart with how he'd treated me that night in the yard before he'd left. Then Uncle Samuel had died, and I'd been so fucking lost. By the time I'd met Karen, I was desperate for love and so fucking lonely she hadn't had to do much to get my attention.

I'd known since high school that I was bisexual. I'd always found beauty in both the male and female forms, but I'd never been open about it. The one constant throughout my life had been the fact that everyone left me, so I hadn't wanted to risk the club finding out about my perversion and tossing me out.

I didn't want to be alone, dammit, so I'd tolerated Karen's bullshit even when it had escalated to physical violence. All to appear normal to my club brothers, and to have someone to come home to.

Then Bomber had come back, and he'd gotten me remembering, thinking. I had to admit, I'd had one foot out the door for months. But I hadn't wanted to risk her temper by breaking up with her, and it'd seemed simpler to just wait her out. Wait for her to get tired of me and leave, just like everyone else had.

Scrubbing a hand over my face, I groaned while I silently cursed myself to hell and back. I needed to man the fuck up. A whole lot of things were gonna change when I got outta here, starting with selling the house. Assuming Scout would let me stay with the Charons, I'd move back into the clubhouse and work my ass off to earn his forgiveness. Get back to basics. Re-earn my place in the club. Maybe even see where things could go with Bomber.

Chapter 6

Bank

By the time I was sitting in an interview room waiting on Tepes, I was in a hell of a mood. The more time I stewed in my own thoughts, the worse I felt. I'd been such a fucking fool. When the door opened to reveal an older, well-dressed man, I was grateful for the distraction. He wore a suit like a man used to wearing one and had an air of authority around him that I had to respect. Hopefully, this was the lawyer Bomber had gotten me, and he knew what the fuck he was doing.

"Sean Arista from Echelon Protection. I'm here to represent you for your arraignment. Do you prefer Bank or Justin?"

Not hearing the name I'd expected, I went on the defensive, sitting back with my arms folded as I glared his way. "I was told to wait for some guy named Tepes."

Sean winced then gave me a tight, professional smile. "That's what they called me in the Marines."

Great. Another former military man. I really was the odd one out wherever I went.

When I didn't offer up anything, he cleared his throat and spoke again, "Let's get the basics out of the way. What were you doing in one of the worst neighborhoods in Philly in the middle of the night?"

I liked that he seemed to be a straight shooter. I kept my arms crossed as I gave the guy a summary of my fucked-up night.

"My girlfriend—well, ex-girlfriend now—planned a trip away for us. When she snuck out of our hotel room last night, I got suspicious and followed her. Figured she was cheating on me, but no, the bitch was delivering drugs."

"So, you knew nothing about the drugs prior to following her?"

Clenching my jaw for a moment, I shook my head. "No fucking clue. Bitch set me up."

He raised an eyebrow, "How, exactly, did she set you up if she was unaware of you following her?"

Fury raced through my blood and before I knew what I was doing, I slammed my fists against the tabletop, keeping my gaze locked with his as I started to speak. "After she handed over the drugs, she demanded her payment. Karen wasn't after cash. No, she wanted them to kill me. If you can get hold of my phone, you'll see the message she sent me, saying she was in trouble and needed me to save her. Gave a different location from the one we were at, though. Bitch was gonna have me offed!"

Rage had roughened my voice, my body nearly vibrating with anger as I thought about all that Karen had done to me while Sean made some notes.

"Do you know why she'd have done that? How long were you and Karen together? I'll also need her last name and date of birth, if you know it."

Forcing myself to breathe deeply, I reined in my emotions and leaned back in my chair as I rubbed a palm over my face.

"Karen Klenig, date of birth is April 16th, 1987. We were together for three years, but it wasn't exactly a happy relationship. Been thinking of cutting her loose lately. Maybe she got wind of that."

Not entirely true, but I couldn't handle this man knowing exactly how weak I'd been with her. He made some more notes. "What were you doing when you were arrested?"

"I'd just received the text and was trying to wrap my head around the fact my girlfriend wanted me dead badly enough she'd arranged to have some thugs kill me for her when there was screaming, and everyone went running. As I moved from where I'd been spying on them, a cop grabbed and cuffed me. One of the joys of being a biker... cops automatically assume we're doing somethin' wrong."

I finished with a shrug and crossed my arms over my chest again, taking some comfort from the feel of the patches on my cut against my forearms.

The man sighed like I wasn't telling him anything he wanted to hear. "Got any redeeming qualities I can use to convince the judge not to set your bail too high?"

That had me chuckling. "Redeeming qualities? What? Like I rescue cats from trees or some shit?"

Now he was rolling his eyes at me. "Yeah, or some shit."

He wasn't going to like my answer to this one either.

"The Charon MC is all about helping the underdog, but we don't exactly mind the law when we do. Generally speaking, it's the law that's failed the person we're helping."

Sean rubbed his forehead in a way that reminded me of my Uncle Samuel. He used to get this frustrated look to him when dealing with me too. I'd never been one to say more than I absolutely had to.

"Bank, I need something to work with. I can't go in defending you by saying you're some sort of vigilante superhero. You have to help me help you."

I shrugged one shoulder. Short of making something up, I wasn't entirely sure what he wanted from me.

"My record is clean. Haven't even caught a speeding ticket in about ten years. I live quietly and mind my own business. I work hard and pay my taxes on time. If you're subtly asking if I have any club secrets I'll hand over for my freedom, that's a solid *hell no*. Got my name because I can keep a secret better than a bank vault. I won't ever turn on my club."

Bomber

I hadn't checked any luggage, so the moment I could get free of the plane, I rushed toward the exit. Static had messaged to say he would be waiting out at the pick-up line for me, so that's where I headed.

Despite the circumstances, I had to shake my head with a laugh as I approached the massive beast of a vehicle that stood out against all the sedans like a hooker in church. The big, black SUV reminded me of some of the vehicles I'd had to work on when I was deployed. Well, at least it did until I opened the front passenger door and got a look inside. Getting in, I shoved my bag down into the footwell.

"Damn, brother. You got enough toys in here?"

Every inch of the dash was covered with high-tech gadgets.

He shrugged, "They come in handy. Wish we'd had even half this shit over there."

I nodded as I scanned the car again before I switched my attention to the man I hadn't seen in six months. He hadn't changed much, aside from letting his hair grow out a little.

"Anything new with Bank?"

"His arraignment is scheduled for one, so we got time to get there before it starts."

I nodded, relieved I'd made it here in time to at least be in the room with him.

Silence filled the car for a few moments before Static cleared his throat. "This man, he's not just a club brother to you, is he?"

I chuckled. Guess I was wrong regarding what my squadron had assumed about me.

"At the moment, he's only a club brother."

"But you're feeling him. Is he the reason you never went home between deployments?"

I turned from looking out the window to him. "You're not pulling your punches today, are you?"

He shook his head, a serious look on his face as he continued to focus on the road. "Put a lot on the line to get your boy the help he needed. Least you can do is tell me why you're calling in a favor for him."

Rubbing a palm over the back of my neck, I looked up into the cloudy sky outside.

"Yeah, I guess you're right. Last time I came home was about six and a half years ago. We had a moment, but I pushed too hard, too fast and he ran. Then I got deployed and by the time I was next back stateside, I didn't want to deal with the situation, so I stayed away."

He frowned. "Not sure he's gay. I mean, he's with that chick, isn't he?"

That had me huffing out a short laugh, "Static, it ain't black and white. There are all sorts of shades of gray between being gay and straight. I've always known I'm gay. Women have never aroused me like men do. And no one has ever caught my eye like Bank. From the first time he came into the clubhouse, he had my attention. He's flirted with me in the past, and when I had my hand on his cock, it was hard as stone. I ain't pining away for a straight man here. And I don't intend to pounce on the man now. Karen's been doing a number on him for fucking years. Guessing he'll need a little time to heal before he's ready to get serious with me. But I ain't leaving him again, no matter how many times he freaks out and pushes me away."

"How can you be so fucking sure he's feeling you the same way you're feeling him?"

I turned back to him, and he looked my way for a moment before moving his focus to the road again.

"Because he messaged me. When things went to shit, he reached for me. Not the club, me. Would have made more sense to call Keys or the general line to Athena Security, but he didn't. He texted me when he heard Karen threaten him, then later he used his one call from lock-up to call me. That's how I know."

We pulled into the courthouse parking lot.

"How's your club gonna handle that?"

I shrugged as I grabbed my bag and opened the door. "They know about my preferences, and no one's ever batted an eye over it. I doubt we'll cop any trouble over it, but I'm sure that's why Bank freaked out on me all those years ago. We got a lot to talk about once I get his ass outta this place."

Once out of the vehicle, I walked beside Static, who had his phone out, reading texts as we made our way inside.

"Follow me and we'll head into the public gallery area. We're a little early, so might have to sit through a case or two before your boy's on. Looks like Tepes found some evidence that's got him excited. Guess time will tell if it's enough."

Slipping through the door, I sat beside Static toward the back and watched as a couple other men went through the process of being arraigned. What evidence could he have found? They'd been in a shitty part of town. If there had been CTTV footage, Jacie would have found it by now.

Before I got too far down that rabbit hole, Bank came in from a side door. Fuck, he looked bad. Shoulders slumped, head down, he was a man at the end of his rope. I prayed Tepes could get him off. That I'd have the chance to take Bank home with me and help build him back up.

Before the judge could say a thing, the DA stood and requested a word up at the bench. I looked to Static, but he was frowning as much as I was, so clearly, he had no clue what was going on either. We were too far away to hear what they were saying but the judge raised an eyebrow and didn't look happy with the DA. The man who I guessed was Tepes had a shocked expression but grinned as he turned back toward Bank.

The judge proclaimed all charges had been dropped and that Justin Lewis was free to go.

"Fuck, he did it! He fuckin' did it."

I ignored Static's words as I stood and rushed to the front of the room, to where Tepes was guiding a very shocked looking Bank toward me.

"Bank!"

He blinked a few times before focusing on me. He shook his head like he still couldn't believe what had just happened.

Static grabbed my arm as I reached for Bank. "Not here, Bomber."

The four of us moved out of the courtroom and into the hallway before Tepes spoke. "Follow me."

He led us into a small waiting room that was empty.

"Someone videoed the entire deal and delivered the video footage to me. The DA knew I had it, but I hadn't lodged it yet. Not sure what the DA knows in all of this, but I suggest you two get back to Texas as soon as you can. No need to risk him changing his mind." He adjusted his tie. "I'll go get Bank's things from lock-up and give you two a moment. Static will watch the door to make sure you are not disturbed."

I turned to the men who'd helped free Bank. "Thank you both. Static, could you book us a flight back to Houston while I have a chat with Bank?"

He smirked and gave me a wink. "Sure, brother."

Then I was alone with Bank, who seemed to still be in shock. "I'm free?"

Unable to stand it a moment longer, I wrapped my palm around the back of his neck and yanked him in against me, until our foreheads touched. "All charges are dropped, Bank. You're free as a bird."

A shudder ran through him as he moved to drop his head to my shoulder and wrapped his arms around my waist. I banded mine around his back, holding him to me as he shuddered, and wetness hit my neck.

"I got you, boy." I turned my face and pressed a kiss to his temple. Fuck, he felt right in my arms. I prayed he wouldn't keep fighting me, the attraction between us.

After a few minutes, he drew a deep breath and pulled back. I loosened my hold but didn't release him completely. I wasn't ready to let go yet.

"I'm leaving Karen."

A shot of fury coursed through me. "Damn straight you are. Whole club's looking for her. She'll get what's coming to her for what she's done."

"Is the club going to come for me too?"

I frowned at him. "I came for you, Bank, but with the entire club's blessing."

He shook his head, "Not what I meant. Is Scout wanting me to leave? Am I gonna get a beat down if I return to Bridgewater?"

Fuck, but he broke my heart wide open. "Karen's been filling your head with lies and bullshit for years. You didn't do a damn thing wrong here. You are a fully-patched-in brother of the Charon MC, Bank. You always will be. The entire club is at your back on this. And if you can't trust in that, trust that I'll be standing beside you from here on out. I'll be your shield, Justin. I vow to you, I will keep you protected from any threat."

I shifted, forcing him to back up until he was against the wall. Then I wrapped my palm around the front of his throat just like I had all those years ago. When his gaze lowered to my mouth, I took it as a green light and slammed my lips over his. The kiss was a statement, a claim.

He was mine.

Chapter 7

Bank

In a state of shock, I was barely aware of a damn thing going on around me.

All charges had been dropped, so I was a free man.

Bomber had claimed me with a kiss so scorching hot, my lips still tingled from the contact.

Seeming to know how out of it I was, Bomber guided me every step of the way. He checked us both in at the airport, then handled the TSA agent and got us onto a plane. It wasn't until I stepped out of George Bush International Airport into the Houston humidity that reality wiped away the fog and I jerked to a stop and panic rose up.

I wanted to trust what Bomber had said about how the club would have my back, but I remembered what had happened to Eagle and Runt. Eagle copped a beat down for not keeping Silk safe when he'd been guarding her. Well, that was the official reason. We all knew it was really because he'd touched Silk, a daughter of the club, while he was still a prospect, so yeah, that was different than what I'd done. And Runt had been a little snitch who was taken out for reporting to a rival club what we'd been doing.

My situation was unlike both of those, but I'd seen how the

club doled out justice.

A large, rough palm wrapped around the back of my neck, and it settled me enough I could take a couple deep breaths.

"Everything is gonna work out, Bank. No one in the club is mad at you, I promise."

He squeezed before releasing his hold and nudging me toward the parking lot. My steps slowed as we approached Bomber's big, black Harley. Fuck, I didn't have my bike.

"You got a problem riding with me?"

His voice held a hint of emotion. Fear, maybe.

I shook my head. "Never been on the back of someone else's bike before."

Nerves shot through my system along with a good dose of arousal. My cock twitched in my jeans at the thought of being pressed up against Bomber for the long ride back to Bridgewater.

Next thing I knew, Bomber's big hand was wrapped around the front of my throat again and he was staring into my eyes with an intensity that stole my breath.

"You won't ever ride on the back of anyone's bike but mine. I don't fucking share, boy."

"I ain't giving up my sled, Bomber. I won't be riding bitch on club runs."

With a growl, he leaned in and took my mouth with his. His lips firm and demanding, so addictive I didn't even attempt to resist. I couldn't. This man rendered me useless with his kisses.

When he pulled back, we were both breathing heavy.

"Fuckin' hell, now we both gotta ride with hard-ons. I'm taking you home, boy. Then I'm gonna claim what's mine. You got a problem with that?"

While I'd been in lock-up, I decided to see where things with

Bomber could go, but I figured it'd be a slow burn thing. Of course, that was before he'd started melting my mind with his kisses. My cock throbbed for this man.

"No problem."

His grin was feral and the glint in his eyes would have scared me if I'd thought about it too long.

"Good. Then get your sweet ass on my bike and let's go."

Before I could respond, he turned and opened a saddle bag. "Give me your pack."

Somehow, Bomber's friends had managed to get my stuff from the hotel and had given it to me when we'd left the courthouse. I hadn't traveled with much, so it all easily fit into something I could carry on to the plane. Handing the backpack over, Bomber made fast work of stashing it away before he handed me a helmet then mounted his ride. I had to bite the inside of my cheek to stop myself from making a sound in appreciation of how good he looked. The man was such a work of art in clothes, I could only imagine how good he was going to look out of them.

He turned his head to give me a raised eyebrow, "You coming or what?"

Fuck. I wish we could do something that would end with both of us coming right about now.

The smirk he gave me told me he knew what I was thinking and had heat racing across my cheeks. I busied myself buckling the helmet before, holding my breath, I slid onto the seat behind Bomber's big body. His scent, still the same as it had been all those years ago, surrounded me, instantly both calming and arousing me. Bomber started up his bike and once I wrapped my arms around his waist, we took off.

We were on the highway out of Houston when I got brave and slipped my hand under Bomber's cut. His muscles jumped under my palm but he didn't pull my hand out so I pushed my luck, tugging at his shirt until I could get under that too. Sliding my palm across the warm, soft skin over his hard abs had my cock jerking uncomfortably against my jeans and leaking precum that would hopefully not soak though my boxers to my jeans by the time we got to Bridgewater.

Bomber's fingers stroked along my forearm, and I tensed, thinking he'd pull my arm away, but instead he pressed against my hand, flattening it so I covered more of his skin. Then he gripped my thigh for a few moments before returning his palm to the handlebars.

Fuck, this was really happening. I was riding bitch behind Bomber, had my hand on his bare skin. And soon, I'd have much more of him on me... in me.

Excitement thrummed through me and for the first time in years, a genuine smile pulled at my lips.

Bomber

Damn, but my boy was a tease. When his hand, cool from the wind against us as we rode, slipped under my cut, I wasn't sure what he was doing. At first, I'd figured he was just trying to keep them warm out of the wind, but then he tugged at my shirt and had gone under that too. His callused fingers slid over the sensitive skin of my stomach until I placed my hand over his to press it against me. Fuck, but it felt great having his hand on my bare skin.

Thoughts of what kind of lover Bank would be kept my cock hard as stone and leaking for the rest of the ride back to my place. I wouldn't be able to take things slowly with him, like

I'd originally wanted. I'd thought he'd need time to himself for a while, to heal from Karen, but that was not the vibe Bank was giving off. Nope, he was feeling the same way as me. The chemistry between us was off the charts and by the time I pulled into my driveway, my only thought was how quickly could I get him naked and under me.

Hitting the garage door opener, I rode into the large space and parked next to Bank's bike. Our rides looked good next to each other. Right. Bank's palm slid out from under my shirt, and I shivered at losing his warmth. By the time the garage door rolled shut, I had my helmet off and was staring hard at my boy. Bank's gaze didn't leave mine as he fumbled with his own helmet, nearly dropping the thing before he settled it on the handlebar.

"If you're not ready for this, tell me now and we can go to the clubhouse. Because if you enter my home, I ain't gonna let you leave until you know exactly who you belong to. You get me?"

Bank's Adam's apple bobbed as he swallowed then his eyelids lowered and a sexy as fuck look softened his features.

"I'm ready, Bomber. I want this—want you."

"Follow me."

I spun on my heel and unlocked the door into the house. Once inside, I stood holding it open, waiting for Bank to follow. The younger man had a fluid grace to his movements I'd always found mesmerizing. I couldn't fucking wait to have him under me, to see how he moved when I was deep inside him.

The moment he cleared the door, I shoved it closed and had him pinned against it, my palm around his throat, where I could feel his racing pulse.

"You're done with that bitch."

I hadn't worded it as a question, but he still nodded, "Definitely done. Already decided to sell the house. Can't even think about stepping foot in that place again. Gonna live at the clubhouse for a while."

I cut off anything else he was going to say with a growl, "You'll move in here. If we're doing this, it's all in."

He shook his head, a little steel creeping into his gaze, "No, I can't give you that. Not yet. I need to be me for a while. I feel this crazy chemistry we have, and I want to explore it but I don't want to rush it and risk burning it out too soon. Or for this to be just a rebound thing and be over before it gets started."

I wanted to order him to stay here, to never leave my damn sight, especially while Karen was still on the loose with a damn gun I knew she wasn't afraid to use. But I could respect his reasons. I fucking loved that he wanted to give us a real go.

"You give me tonight, I'll take you to the clubhouse tomorrow. But today and tonight, you're mine."

He nodded, the pulse under my fingers jumping. I slammed my mouth down onto his, thrusting my tongue in when his lips parted on a groan. His hands landed on my hips, tugging more of my shirt out so he could get underneath. But it wasn't enough. I wanted him fucking naked. Wanted to be naked.

I tore my mouth from his and shrugged out of my cut, carefully laying it over the back of the couch. Without me needing to say a word, Bank followed my lead, placing his cut over top of mine. The moment he lifted his hand, I was back on him. His shirt ripped as I yanked it up and over his head, then I was at his belt. By the time I had his zipper lowered, he was shoving at the waistband. He toed off his boots and kicked off his jeans, quickly standing in front of me naked except for his boxer-briefs. His skin told a story I'd hoped hadn't been true.

"Fuck, Bank."

My gaze trailed over the bruises and cuts. Goddammit, he might have more scars than me and I'd been to fucking war. Normally, I had a rule about harming a woman but when I got my hands on that bitch, all bets would be off.

Bank had curled into himself, crossing his arms over his chest and keeping his eyes down, no doubt wondering if he shouldn't dress again and leave. With two strides, I was back in close to him. With all the gentleness I could muster, I held his face between my palms and tilted his head up until he was forced to look at me.

"Never again, boy. I will never allow anyone to lay a damn finger on you again, you hear me?"

He swallowed, his eyes glazed with moisture, but he didn't say a word.

"She will never get near you again, and I'll make damn sure she pays for what she's done to you."

I could see in his gaze he didn't fully believe me, and I could understand that. I was sure Karen had made all sorts of promises over the time they were together. He would learn I was a man of my word, and that I'd always take care of him.

I lowered my mouth to his, this time gently brushing my lips over his, gently coaxing him to relax, to lower his arms and press himself against me. Without breaking the kiss, I toed off my own boots, kicking them aside. Before I could go for my belt, Bank's hands were there, his deft fingers tugging and pulling until my pants went loose. Pulling away a step, I reached for the hem of my shirt, stripping it over my head while Bank yanked my jeans down. Cheeky boy took my briefs with them, so I was naked once I stepped out of my pants.

I palmed my hard cock, stroking it as I watched Bank shimmy out of his own underwear. His dick was as hard as mine, as evidenced by the wet patch on his boxer briefs. He'd gotten as horny as I had on the ride from Houston.

He licked his lips and my attention zeroed in on his mouth, memories of that night in the clubhouse yard floating across my mind.

"Want your mouth on me, boy. Get over here and on your knees."

Unlike last time, this time he didn't run away. Without taking his gaze from mine, he fell to his knees and rested his palms on my thighs. When I stroked myself again, his eyes dropped to the action, and that pink, wet tongue of his made another trip over his lower lip.

"You ever sucked a cock before, boy?"

He nodded.

"You ever had one up that fine ass of yours?"

He nodded again. That sent a mix of emotions through me. I was possessive enough to hate that some other man had been inside him, but it meant this wasn't new to him. I wasn't risking being a novelty and nothing more.

I shifted my grip, so my cockhead was aimed at his lush mouth.

"Open up and take me deep, boy."

His lips parted and his fingers dug into my thighs as I pressed inside his mouth for the first time.

Wet heat engulfed me and when he swirled his tongue around the tip, lapping the precum from my slit, I saw double for a few seconds.

"Fuck!"

Releasing my dick, I ran my hands into his hair, gripping fistfuls before I pulled him in toward me, compelling him to swallow more of my length. I didn't force him all the way down, only guided him, but he knew what I wanted and with a hum, he took me all the way to his throat. The feel of him swallowing around me weakened my damn knees. Then he slid one hand from my thigh to cup my balls. He gently rolled them and fuck, I hadn't gotten this turned on by a blow job since my teens.

"Damn, but you're lethal, boy."

I pumped into his mouth for a few minutes, enjoying every moment until I needed more. Pulling him off me, I dragged him to his feet and slammed my mouth over his, hard and fast. The kiss was wet and held zero finesse, but it didn't matter— he was as fucking horny as I was, and I needed to take him.

"In the bedroom. I want your ass in the air."

A shudder ran through him, and his lids lowered again, in that dazed, sexy way he had. I wished I could shove him against the wall and fuck him here and now, but we weren't at that stage yet. Once he was used to being fucked on the regular and was comfortable with my size, we could do that. Assuming he enjoyed a little burn with his pleasure.

Chapter 8

Bank

Grateful I'd been given a tour at Bomber's housewarming party, I knew where to go and didn't waste time as I rushed up the hallway toward Bomber's bedroom. My cock throbbed with need, and I knew it wasn't going to take much to push me over the edge, so I didn't dare stroke myself to ease the ache. No way was I going to come before I had Bomber deep inside me.

Turning into his room, I glanced over my shoulder to see Bomber was several steps behind me, his gaze glued to my butt. I clenched in response before I rushed into the room and basically dove onto his bed, laying on my front, with my knees tucked under me so my ass was in the air and the first thing he'd see when he came through the door.

All the bruises and shit from Karen's last attack still ached, but they were easy to ignore when it was so much more delicious to focus on the anticipation of having Bomber's big hands on me, his thick cock inside my ass.

"Now that's a sight I could easily get used to. You comfortable in that position?"

His voice was so deep and gravelly with arousal, a shiver went down my spine and landed in my cock, having it twitch and leak more precum.

"Please, Bomber. Stop teasing me already."

His chuckle wasn't overly reassuring but he moved to the nightstand and opened the drawer, grabbing out some lube and condoms that he tossed near me on the bed.

"How long since you've had a cock up your ass, boy?"

"Years. Not since before Karen—"

His growl cut off my words. "Don't want to hear her name, especially not in this room."

I could do that. I would happily never see or speak of her again.

"It's been over three years since I've been with a man."

He nodded and moved to stand behind me, and the moment he was out of my sight I tensed. A reflex now after the years of Karen's violence. I jerked and nearly bolted from the bed when his hand softly touched between my shoulder blades.

"Shh, you're safe with me."

His big hand ran down my spine before he used both palms to learn every inch of my back. With every gentle glide up or down, I relaxed more until with a moan, I melted into the comforter.

"That's it. I got you, boy. Trust me to take care of you."

My eyes stung at his words, at how much I wanted what he offered. The next pass down, he dipped lower, closer to my anus, which clenched in anticipation. Keeping up his stroking with one hand, he took the other away. When I heard the lube bottle lid pop open, I had to force my muscles to stay relaxed. It had been so long since I'd felt a man's touch, had a thick dick deep inside me. Hell, it'd been months since I had any sort of sex. And I'd never felt so needy as I did now. I desperately wanted the connection to Bomber that having sex would bring.

Then his fingers were there, slick with lube. He circled my hole, rubbing and teasing until the muscles relaxed enough that he could slip a finger inside. I bucked against the invasion as I gripped at the bedding in attempt to hold still. As he added a second finger and began to pump in and out, his other hand continued to trail up and down my spine. The gentle touch mixed with the eroticism of him finger fucking my ass had me panting in no time.

"Please, Bomber."

"I'm not Bomber when we're like this. You call me David when I'm lovin' on you."

I could do that. Hell, I was so fucking turned on right now, I'd have happily called him Sir.

"David, please stop teasing me."

He pulled free from my body, the friction leaving me trembling.

"Roll over while I go clean up. I wanna look into your eyes the first time I take you."

A shudder ran through me, shaking me to my soul as he moved away and into the bathroom. As the water turned on, I moved up the mattress so when I rolled over, my head was on the pillow. Nerves had me on edge, unsure what to do while I waited. Thankfully, he didn't take long and as soon as he re-entered the room, my gaze was glued to the sight he made. He was beautifully built, and he'd aged well. Like his hair and beard, his chest hair had gone mostly gray too. He had strong arms, wrapped in muscle, his abs were defined and his thighs and legs, a work of art.

A sigh slipped free before I could stop it, and he smirked. "Glad you like what you see."

I lifted a shoulder, "What's not to like? You gotta know you look good."

His gaze trailed over my body, leaving a wave of heat in its wake. "You're not so bad yourself."

With all the black and blues that currently covered me, I doubted I was much to look at currently. Maybe once I healed from Karen's last attack, I'd be able to believe his words.

That had me thinking about the skunk that sprayed her, and the one baby that survived but before I could go down that path, Bomber was climbing onto the bed and instantly had my full attention. He crawled up until I was caged beneath him, and his face was above mine.

"Can't tell you how long I've imagined this moment. You under me, here in my bed."

Before I could think of a response, he lowered down to kiss me, his hard cock rubbing up against mine, making me moan and arch up under him as I wrapped my palms around his biceps to hold on. His beard was soft against my skin as he left my mouth and trailed kisses over my jaw and down my neck. He nibbled on my collarbone before he pulled back to kneel between my spread thighs. He reached over and grabbed a pillow. Guessing what he wanted, I lifted my butt up and he tucked it under me, raising my ass to the right angle.

Bomber

Reaching over for a condom, I tore it open and had myself sheathed in moments. I couldn't wait to get my cock into his tight hole. Claim him as mine. Grabbing the lube next, I slathered a good amount onto my dick. You could never have too much lube for anal.

As I wiped my palm off on the hand towel I'd brought in

from the bathroom, I ran my gaze over my boy. It was starting to get dim in the room, the sun on its way to setting, so all the marks that marred his body were hidden by shadows and he was sexy as fuck. A male in his prime, spread out and prepped for me to take as I wanted.

Grabbing my cock around the base with one hand, I lined the head up with his slick hole. I didn't know what to watch as I breached his ass for the first time. I wanted to see his face, watch his expression as I owned him, but I also wanted to witness how his body sucked me in. Welcomed me inside.

I ended up flicking my gaze between the two until I was buried balls deep, then I gripped his hips and focused completely on his face as I pulled back and thrust in again. He was so fucking tight, he was strangling my cock and I wasn't going to last long. But I wasn't worried, I had a feeling that with Bank, I wouldn't ever need long to recover before I'd be rock hard again and able to go another round.

When I bottomed out on the next stroke, making sure I hit his prostate, he arched under me and tightened his grip on the sheets. How he looked in this moment was something I'd remember forever... the way sweat glistened on his skin, the half lidded, dazed look in his eyes. The way his body took me inside. He was fucking perfect and I knew this was it. He was the only one I'd ever share this with. I'd do whatever I had to keep him with me.

Releasing my hold on his right hip, I moved to grip his cock. A shudder ran through him and the way his ass clenched around my dick had me seeing stars for a moment. Tightening my fist around his thick length, I started to stroke him in time with my thrusts.

"You're mine, boy. Every inch of you is fucking mine."

He nodded but didn't say anything, so I growled, "Tell me,

give me the words."

"Yours. I'm yours. Only yours."

With another growl, I thrust faster into him, tugged on his cock harder until his body shuddered again and his erection kicked in my grip a moment before ropes of white cum shot out to splatter his torso. The moment he was done coming, I leaned over him, wrapping my palm around the front of his throat as I slammed my mouth over his, claiming his mouth as my own orgasm barreled through me and I filled the condom with my seed, wishing like hell I wasn't wearing the damn thing.

"Next time, I ain't wearing a glove. I want to fill you up, know you have my cum deep inside you."

"We need—"

I shook my head. "I'm clean. Haven't fucked anyone since my last medical."

His expression dropped, sadness creeping in. "I haven't been with anyone other than Ka— um, *her* for years, but I've got no clue who she's been with, so yeah, I need to go get tested to be sure."

I liked he already remembered I didn't want her name to taint our bedroom, and I agreed that it was probable that the bitch hadn't been faithful.

"I'll take you in tomorrow to get it done. I want to take you bare, feel you with nothing between us."

He wrapped his arms around my shoulders, pulling me back down for a kiss. This one was sweeter, gentle, and I reveled in the comfort of it.

Chapter 9

Bank

The next morning, I was a mass of nerves. We were going to the clubhouse. Normally, it would be fairly empty on a Thursday morning, but I knew word had spread about what Karen did and how Bomber brought me home, so I suspected I'd be greeted by more than a few of the club brothers.

Bomber came up and gripped my shoulder as I drank the last of my coffee.

"Come on, Bank. Let's get this over with. You're all up in your head for no good reason. The club has your back on this. No one blames you."

I nodded but didn't really believe him. After I rinsed out the mug, I followed Bomber to the garage, both of us grabbing our cuts from the back of the couch as we passed by.

"Do you mind if I take my own bike?"

He shook his head. "Can't lie and say I didn't enjoy the fuck out of having you behind me yesterday, but I get the need to ride your own sled."

Thankful my keys were in the bag of my stuff Bomber's buddies had gathered from the hotel, I went over to my bike, running my hand over the leather. If I didn't get a chance to take my bike out for even a day, I felt it. And with all the shit that had gone down in the last couple days, I really needed a ride.

"Is Scout waiting on us or can we go for a cruise first?"

He hit the door opener and waited for it to finish rumbling before he answered. "We got time to take a scenic route."

With a grin, I finished gearing up and mounted my bike before I rolled out of the garage and waited for Bomber to join me. Then we were off, side by side, heading out of Bridgewater to the open roads.

Twenty minutes later, we pulled into the clubhouse. I was still nervous but much calmer after the ride. After I parked next to Bomber, we dismounted, took our helmets off and strode toward the front door. Whether Bomber was right or not about how the club was going to react, I wanted it over with.

As soon as I passed through the door, Scout and Mac stood from one of the tables and headed our way. Scout marched straight up to me, gripped my shoulder tightly and stared me in the eye.

"You doing good, brother?"

My throat clogged with emotion for a moment, forcing me to clear it before I could speak. "Yeah, I'm okay. Listen, Scout, I had no fucking clue she'd been dealing, I swear."

He shook his head, cutting me off. "I know you well enough to know you weren't in on her shit. And even if I didn't, I've seen all the video feeds Jacie and Keys found, and it's clear what went down. I got brothers out looking for the bitch. She'll pay for pulling this shit."

He released my shoulder as I nodded, not sure what else to say.

Bomber broke the moment when he wrapped his palm around the back of my neck as he spoke.

"See? Told you the club had your back."

Scout frowned as he looked between me and Bomber, "What the fuck else would we do when a brother is in trouble?"

Mac stepped in closer, joining the conversation. "At a rough guess, he figured we'd boot him to the curb or deliver a beat down. That bitch did a number on you, brother. You're a Charon. We will *always* have your back."

I nodded again, feeling a fool.

Scout shook his head as he mumbled under his breath before he glanced over to the bar. "I need a fucking drink."

We all followed him over and once the prospect manning it passed out glasses to us all, Scout nodded back toward the tables.

"Take a seat so we can talk."

No sooner had I settled into my seat than Keys came out from the hallway that led to the offices, laptop in hand, and moved straight toward us.

Scout looked to him as he sat. "What have you found?"

"No sign of Karen yet, but I've picked up on something else. There's a handful of Mexicans who've been hanging around. Wouldn't normally think much of it, but they seem to be focused on Marie's Cafe, and it's not that far-fetched to think Karen was transporting drugs for a Mexican cartel." He turned to me. "You know anything about who she's been seeing? Who she's running drugs for?"

I shook my head. "I have no fucking clue, brother. I'm sorry. First I knew was after I'd followed her and saw her hand that shit over. I wasn't close enough to see markings on the packages or anything. Tepes, my lawyer, didn't mention anything in my meetings with him, either."

Keys frowned as he nodded and tapped away at the keyboard. "I'll see what I can dig up but thinking we're gonna have to wait till we get our hands on Karen. Although, if those boys try anything, we'll grab them and see what they have to say. I don't want to start a war with a fucking cartel if we don't have to."

Scout pulled out his phone as he spoke. "We need extra guards on Marie's Cafe and anywhere else the old ladies are. Ain't having a fucking repeat of that mess with the Ice Riders."

Last year, the Ice Riders MC, a club from up in Boston, decided to get our attention by storming Marie's Cafe and holding a fucking gun to her pregnant belly. Didn't end well for those fuckers. With some help from some allies up north, we wiped the club out of existence.

Mac rose from his seat. "I'll head over there now to cover things till you get shit organized."

He strode to the front door as Scout stood and moved toward the hall that led to his office, no doubt to call in a couple of the enforcers to join the prospects on guard duty.

I stared into my drink as my mind raced. Had Karen really been in bed with a cartel? How the fuck had I not seen any signs? Of course, I'd been doing my best to avoid her for months now, working as much as I could, since that was one of the few things I could do that she didn't argue about.

I needed to get my shit outta that house.

I glanced up to Bomber. "You wanna help me go pack up my shit and move it here?"

He nodded but before he spoke, Keys cut in, "Use one of the club cages. I'll see if anyone is around to help."

I shook my head. "Thanks, but there's no need. There's not much I want to grab, so it won't take us long."

Bomber

Pulling up to the house Bank shared with Karen had me on edge. I was fairly certain there was nothing but bad memories here for my boy, and I couldn't wait to gather his shit and get him away from here for the last time. I'd happily pay someone to come clean out all her shit so the place could be sold.

I wasn't going to fight Bank on wanting to live at the clubhouse… for now. But I knew it wouldn't be long before I had him moved in with me.

Bank turned off the engine then with a huff, shoved the door open and got out. I followed his lead, letting him stay in his head as I took in everything around us. Until Karen was located, I'd be on high alert. I wasn't sure if Bank knew, but Scout had put a couple brothers on duty watching this place, so it was unlikely she was here or they'd have reported it in.

That didn't stop me from pulling my gun free and having it ready when Bank unlocked the door and shoved it open, then cursed. "Fuck me."

Without thought, I moved to stand in front of Bank, gun up and making a sweep of the chaos that was within the house.

"Call Keys, let him know what's going on. I'm going to check to see if anyone is still here."

Before he could argue, I headed off, clearing each room I found. The entire house had been ransacked. Nothing was left untouched. I hoped Bank didn't have any family heirlooms in among this shit because I wasn't sure anything had survived intact. Lighting this place up would have done less damage.

By the time I made it back to the living room, Bank was just hanging up his phone.

"Keys said it must have happened last night. The prospect who was supposed to be watching this place decided to slip away to do other things. Idiot didn't make it back in time to hand over to the next guard, so he got busted."

I winced. That man wasn't in for a good time. "Now that fucker will get that beat-down you were worried about."

Bank nodded, seeming to be in a bit of a daze. "Keys mentioned something about that."

Tucking my gun away, I moved over to stand in front of Bank, taking his face between my palms I looked him in the eye for a moment before I leaned in and gave him a gentle kiss. By the time I pulled back, he had his hands on my hips and my cock was throbbing for some action, but that wouldn't happen until we got back to the clubhouse. This house was tainted, even more so now it'd been trashed.

Dropping my hands away, I reluctantly stepped away. "Do you have anything special you want to look for before we go?"

He shook his head. "Nothing here that can't be replaced."

"Let's get back to the clubhouse, then. No sense being here now."

With a hand on his lower back, I guided him through the front door and to the cage, getting him settled before I returned to lock up the front door. Once finished, I turned back toward the car but paused when I caught a glimpse of movement at the side of the house that had my instincts thrumming.

Pulling my gun out once more, I took off, aware that Bank was getting out of the vehicle behind me but not wanting to risk losing my target by stopping to tell him what I was doing. The side gate was open, and I raced through, keeping my gaze alert for any movement. The sounds of wood creaking and a few grunts let me know they'd gone over the back fence. As I ran, I re-holstered my weapon, so I had both hands free to grab the top of the fence to vault over it.

Landing on the other side in a crouch, I sprang forward and

tackled Karen down to the dirt. She didn't have any training, so fumbled with the fence, falling at a bad angle on the other side. She'd probably twisted an ankle or something similar, not that I gave a fuck as I grabbed her arm and wrenched it up behind her roughly, then pressed a knee to her back to make sure she stayed the fuck down.

"Don't move, bitch."

She mumbled something, but I didn't give a fuck what she had to say. I pulled my phone out and called Keys.

"What's up now?"

Couldn't really blame the man for assuming the worst, since every time I'd rung lately it'd been to tell him bad news.

"Just caught our little runaway. I've got her contained in the backyard of the house to the rear of Bank's old place. Wouldn't mind someone coming to pick up the garbage so I don't have to put it in the car with my boy."

"Excellent. Someone'll be there in a couple minutes. Hang tight."

There was excitement to his tone that almost had me chuckling. This whole situation wasn't just pissing me off.

After ending that call, I called Bank. "Hang at the car, I'll be back there soon. Just waiting on someone to come collect the garbage."

"You got Karen?"

"Yep. So, you stay there so you don't have to deal with her again. Let me handle this."

"Okay."

I didn't like the sound of his tone, but I'd deal with it later.

Karen started to squirm, trying to break free, so I yanked her arm higher until her shoulder nearly popped out of joint.

"Don't test me, bitch. After what you've done, I have no problem hurting you."

"Thought the Charons didn't harm women."

"We don't. Drug dealing pieces of shit who set up our brothers are a different matter entirely."

She stilled for a few seconds before shaking her head and resting it down on the dirt. She knew she'd fucked up and there was a price she'd have to pay.

Chapter 10

Bank

Bomber was in a mood when he finally returned to the cage, so I stayed silent. I was reeling from everything that had happened in the past twenty-four hours. All charges against me had been dropped. Bomber had come for me, brought me home then thoroughly claimed me. My house had been completely trashed, and now Bomber caught Karen and she was being transported to the clubhouse.

As much as I appreciated him saving me from having to deal with her, I was angry to be cut out. I was the one she'd hurt. I should get a shot in on the justice she was to receive.

When Bomber parked in the clubhouse lot, I jumped out of the vehicle and stormed up the clubhouse. I'd worked myself up to a rage, and I wanted my piece out of Karen.

"Whoa, Bank. Hold up."

I shook off Bomber's grasp before I spun on him.

"I have every right to be involved in dealing with her. I'm the one she wanted dead. The one she landed in lock-up with her bullshit. I should get to be there when she's punished."

Bomber's eyebrows rose and he blinked mutely a few times before with a shake of his head, he spoke, "You're mine, Bank. That makes you mine to protect, and that includes from that viper of a woman in there who's hurt you enough already. I wasn't trying to cut you out of the process, I was trying to fucking protect you from being hurt again."

I stormed over to stand in front of him. "I don't—" I stopped short, my anger vanishing under the weight of memories of all the times Karen had beat on me, all the times I had needed someone to step in, but no one was there.

Bomber's hand wrapped around the front of my neck as he liked to do, the pressure calming me even more.

"I wasn't here when she first started attacking you, but I'm damn well here now and I ain't leaving you to the wolves, Bank. I got you on this. Let the club and me deal with her. You never have to see her again. You got questions, let me know and I'll get you answers, but I don't want her to get a chance to sink her claws into your body or your mind ever again."

Tears pricked the back of my eyes, and I blinked like crazy to fight them back. We were in the middle of the clubhouse parking lot, for fuck's sake. Anyone could see us.

"You gonna let me kiss you? Claim you in front of the brothers? Or you gonna make us hide?"

I shook my head as much as I could with his grip on my throat. "Don't wanna hide, but I don't want to be kicked out either."

"I'm gonna need you to tell me who the hell hurt you so bad that's your first thought whenever shit hits the fan, but not right now."

With that, he laid his lips on mine, and my hands automatically went to his hips, holding him in close against me as he claimed me here in front of the prospect manning the door and any brothers who happened to pass through the lot.

Ending the kiss, Bomber kept his forehead against mine. "Let's go upstairs. We'll let the club deal with Karen while we talk, then I'll go see where shit is at, okay?"

I blew out a breath. "Yeah, okay."

Stepping away from each other, I shivered when his warm hand slipped from my throat. I never would have thought such a possessive hold would be something I liked, but with Bomber, it settled me every damn time.

I lowered my eyes as we approached the door, not wanting to see the prospect's face.

Bomber leaned in to speak quietly into my ear, "Don't do that. Don't hide yourself, especially not here."

With a deep inhale, I forced my gaze up, only to see the prospect was scanning the yard as he leaned against the wall, not at all interested in my drama. Chuffing, I shook my head and marched inside, heading straight to the stairs that led up to the bedrooms on the second level. When I got to the top, I headed down to what used to be my room. I hadn't stayed in it for ages so wasn't sure if it was still mine.

I paused when I got to the door, thinking I should have checked with Scout before coming up here.

"You don't have your key anymore?"

I shook my head as I pulled my keys out of my pocket. "I got it. Just wondering if this room was still mine."

"I was gone for six years and mine was still in the same place, and I'm sure yours is too."

Technically, they'd packed up Bomber's stuff and put it downstairs in storage while he was gone so they could use the room for other brothers, then moved it all back up when he let Scout know he was coming home.

Sliding the key in the lock, I tentatively turned it and was relieved when the lock snicked, and the door opened. Shoving it further, I stepped in and grinned at everything the same as I left it. I went over to the closet and was happy to see I'd left some clothes behind. Meant I'd have something to wear in the morning.

The door clicking shut had me closing up the closet and turning to face Bomber.

"You wanted to talk?"

He nodded toward the bed. "Come lie down with me. I want to know your past, why you're so quick to think everyone is gonna fucking reject you the first chance they get."

My gaze flipped between the door and bed as I contemplated my choices. Leave or bare my soul. Ignoring my dilemma, Bomber took his cut off and hung it up on the hook beside the door for just that purpose, then he toed off his boots before he walked over to the bed and laid down, hands behind his head as he focused his piercing green gaze on me.

"I promise there is nothing you can tell me about your past that'll have me walking out that door, Justin. You can trust me to keep your secrets."

My heart rate kicked up the more I thought out baring my soul. I'd never laid it all out for anyone. Not even Scout when I'd prospected then patched in.

"My having a shitty family history ain't exactly a secret."

"You don't go yelling about it from the roof, so yeah, it basically is. I'm sure Keys dug into you, and he knows every little detail, but it's not public knowledge around the club. If it was, I'd have found out about it by now."

Keys would have looked into my history. The blood ran from my face as I thought about what he would have found.

"Bank, get over here now and lie down before you pass the fuck out. Keys does backgrounds on every one of us when we prospect in. He never shares that shit unless it's absolutely necessary. You don't need to worry about what he knows."

To give myself an extra minute, I went over and stripped off my own cut, hanging it carefully with Bomber's. Then I took off my boots, lining them up with his. A pang hit my chest at the domesticity of it. Of how much I liked being close to Bomber. How much I didn't want to lose what was quickly growing between us.

Fuck. It was risky to open up about my past, about how I was brought into the world. But it was a bigger risk to not do it. Instinctively, I knew Bomber wouldn't hang around for long if I refused to tell him anything.

With a deep breath, I turned around to face the man I was rapidly falling for. He now sat on the side of the bed, elbows on his knees as he watched me. My mouth opened and everything just poured out.

"I'm the product of rape. My mom was attacked, and she ended up pregnant. Her parents were religious and refused to allow her to terminate me. But once I was born, she rejected me, wanted nothing to do with me. Neither did my grandparents, so they shipped me off to a relative. Uncle Samuel took care of me, but he wasn't exactly an affectionate man. He'd never been married or even had a long-term relationship. There wasn't a whole lot of warmth in his personality, but he taught me to respect those around me. To never hit a woman. To always work hard at whatever job I was doing. To never leave a debt unpaid."

My throat clogged with emotion, and I couldn't speak anymore. Bomber slowly rose to stand, and my breath hitched in fear of his reaction.

Bomber

No wonder Bank hadn't wanted anyone to know about his past. My poor boy.

I took measured steps until I was close enough I could feel his body heat, then I cupped his face between my palms and stared him straight in the eyes.

"Justin, it's not your fault that your mom was raped. You were a victim in that situation, just like your mom. No one would ever hold that against you."

I leaned in and pressed a gentle kiss to his cold lips before I stroked my hands down his sides until I had his fingers tangled with mine, then I stepped back, drawing him with me until I was back at the bed.

He followed my lead as I guided him to lie down before I settled on the mattress next to him.

"Tell me the rest. Did you have any contact with your mom and grandparents after you moved in with your uncle?"

His gaze shifted from mine to the ceiling, "Not my mom. She made it clear she never wants to even see me again. But my grandparents used to have me over summer break once I was in school. That's how I got to know my little sister."

That had me jerking a little, causing him to return his gaze to me. "I had no idea you had any siblings."

He gave me a sad smile. "I haven't seen her in years now. Not since before I prospected with the Charons. Once my grandparents passed away, there was no way to keep in touch. She's a lot younger than me, so she didn't have her own cell or social media the last time I saw her. I gave her my number and she knows I live here in Bridgewater because that's where Uncle Samuel lived, but I can't contact her. I gotta wait for her to want to contact me. If she ever does."

He'd referred to his uncle in the past tense, but I needed to be sure. "Where's your uncle?"

"Six feet deep. He passed away four years ago. Met Karen six months later."

That made sense. He'd been grieving and feeling lost when that bitch got her claws in him. An easy target, vulnerable and ripe for an abuser to get in her grip. I didn't want him focusing on that shit now, since he was struggling enough as it was.

"What's her name? Your sister."

"Nevaeh. It's heaven spelled backwards because she was my mom's little piece of heaven after suffering through hell. She was married and settled with her husband when she had her. Her life complete." He huffed. "She'd refused to name me, so my grandparents did."

I was glad for that. Who knew what his mom would have named him. Probably Satan or some such bullshit.

"Your mother was wrong, Bank. Her rapist was the criminal... you were an innocent fucking baby."

He nodded and went back to staring at the ceiling, "I know that in theory, but it's hard to change my mindset after so long. My grandparents never mentioned how I was conceived. They were good to me over the years, but they made sure to keep me hidden if Mom came over. She never knew I was there in the summers. If she did, I'm sure she'd have stopped bringing Neveah over while she worked during the day."

I reached out and tangled my fingers with his again, wanting to offer him some comfort. "Did you want to look for her? I'm sure Jacie or Keys could find her location pretty quickly."

He shook his head. "I couldn't handle it if she didn't want to know me. I... fuck. I'm at my quota of people I care about fucking leaving me, okay?"

His eyes were now rimmed with red, but he held the tears back, not letting them flow. Moving until I was over the top of him, I straddled his waist before I leaned forward. When he pressed his palms against my chest, I wrapped a hand around each of his wrists and pinned them to the mattress above his head.

"I claimed you, boy. Last night, I made you mine. I sure as fuck ain't gonna kick you to the curb over shit that's out of your control. I've retired from the Air Force, so I ain't going to up and go on deployment again. I'm gonna stay right here in Bridgewater for the rest of my days, and I'm hoping you'll be by my side for each and every one of them. I get it's gonna take some time for you to believe me, that with your history you can't trust my words yet, but you will. In time, you'll fucking learn I don't break my promises, and I'm promising you right now that I will always be in your corner, at your back."

He cut me off by lifting up and slamming his lips against mine. I caught a glimpse of a tear leaving his eye before they closed, and he stroked his tongue over my lips. With a growl, I sank into the kiss, switching between nibbling at his lips and thrusting my tongue in to dance with his. My cock was throbbing in my jeans, and I could feel his do the same.

Sitting back, I released his wrists so I could grab his shirt and lift it up, needing to feel more of his skin. He took the fabric from me, peeling it up over his head, the play of his muscles mesmerizing me. Fuck, my boy was hot. Leaning down, I took a nipple into my mouth before he had his shirt all the way off and he grunted when I bit down on the tip before I moved to the other side. I couldn't wait for all those bruises and shit to heal up. I hated seeing the evidence of what he'd been suffering through, and I vowed nothing would mar his skin again. Well, except for the odd mark I'd leave behind, but those wouldn't be about hurting him. Those would be about giving him a little sting to add to his pleasure.

Leaning up again, I stripped off my own shirt, liking how he got a dazed look in his eyes as he ran his gaze over my chest and torso. I might be a lot older than my lover, but I was in peak physical condition and could keep up with him.

With a smirk, I went for his jeans. "Please tell me you have condoms in here."

He winced, "If I do, they're years old and wouldn't be any good."

Shifting so I could pull my wallet from my back pocket, I flipped it open and grinned when I hit paydirt. "Got one left." With that, I swung my leg over him so I could stand beside the bed and strip the rest of the way off, desperate to be inside my boy again.

Chapter 11

Bank

Following Bomber's lead, I stood to peel my clothes, not taking my eyes off the man in front of me. Fuck, but he was sexy. As soon as I was naked, I moved in close, running my fingers through the hair on his chest as I nuzzled into his neck, breathing him in as he wrapped his arms around me and held me close. Our erections rubbed together, the friction sending sparks up my spine and making me shiver.

"Want you on your hands and knees, boy. I wanna get in as deep as I can, own every inch of you."

His words had me so turned on, I could barely breathe. I nipped at his collarbone before I pivoted and climbed onto the bed, leaving my knees near the edge so he could stand behind me.

"Lube's in the top drawer."

Hopefully, that was still good. I needed to re-stock my room ASAP.

I turned my head when he started laughing. "Guess someone figured what we'd be doing up here and took care of business."

He tossed a full packet of condoms and a brand-new bottle of lube onto the bed.

"It's not ginger lube, is it? Because I can see Taz pulling that shit."

He picked up the bottle and shook his head. "Nah, just plain ol' lube. I'm sure I could find some ginger if you want it?"

He raised an eyebrow and I growled at him. "No fucking way."

Then he moved to stand behind me, running his palm down my spine and I forgot all about the lube and condoms. Fuck, his touch lit me up. My cock jerked and I flexed my hips in response.

"Shh, Justin, I'll take real good care of you."

His other hand slipped between my thighs, where he cupped my balls, rolling each one in turn until I was moaning, then he grabbed my cock in a tight grip and stroked me a few times while he dribbled the cold lube down my ass crack. He kept up long, slow stokes while with his other hand he toyed with my back entrance, prepping me for his thick erection.

By the time he released my dick to grip my hip as he pressed his broad cockhead against my hole, I was panting. His first thrust deep into my ass hit all the right places, sending a shiver through me. Dropping down onto my elbows, I shifted my weight so I could reach down to palm my dick. Desperate to come already, I knew I wouldn't take long to go over the edge, especially not with how he managed to hit my prostate with every stroke.

I timed my strokes with his, and it wasn't long before I was clamping down on him as I orgasmed, shooting my load over my hand and the sheets. With a growl, he picked up his pace, slamming hard into me over and over again. Pleasure zinged through my bloodstream, making my cock twitch even though I'd just come. With a whimper, I buried my face into the sheets as I shuddered under the onslaught of sensations Bomber was heaping on me.

Then he leaned over and wrapping a palm around the front of my neck, guided me up, so my back was against his front. My head landed on his shoulder, and I reached one arm up and around his head, holding him to me while I wrapped the other one behind his ass, where I could feel the flex and release of his muscles with every thrust.

He twisted his face and nipped at my jaw as he reached his free hand down to palm my semi-hard cock. It was still sensitive from my recent climax, and I hissed out a breath as he stroked me back to a full erection.

"Gonna make you come again before I fill this ass up, boy. Then I'm gonna take you in the shower and see how good you taste."

"Fuck, David."

His dirty talk was nearly enough to have me coming. It was like this man knew my every turn-on on instinct. He continued to fuck me and pump my cock until I was a mindless, whimpering mess. I thrashed against his sweat-slicked body until with a scream, I came again, ropes of cum coating my torso and his hand as I clenched down hard on his cock, pulling his own orgasm from him. He cried out as he jerked, and I felt the warm pulses that meant he was filling the condom.

We really needed to get tested today. I wanted to feel his warmth filling me, knowing I carried some of him inside me during the times we were apart.

Fuck, I was feeling way too much for this man already.

Before I could get too sappy about it all, he pulled free, pressed a kiss to my shoulder, then guided me to the bathroom. He didn't take his hands off me as I turned on the water and got the temperature adjusted. I got one step into the stall before he had me spun around and slammed against the wall, his mouth on mine as the water rushed over both our bodies, taking the mess of cum and lube with it.

This man was fucking insatiable, and unbelievably within minutes, my cock was hard as a rock and weeping. I couldn't remember a time when I'd been able to recover this fast between rounds, but Bomber was pure sex, and I couldn't seem to resist. Especially not when he dropped to his knees and took me into his mouth.

"Fuck!"

Running my hand through his now wet hair, I took hold as I started to pump. He kept his gaze on mine as I thrust a little deeper, until he was swallowing me down to this throat.

"Next time, I want your ass. I need to know how it feels to be inside you that deeply."

He moaned around my cock, and I took it as a yes. Bomber was clearly going to be the more dominant partner in our relationship, but I wouldn't be the bottom every time. Especially after everything Karen had done to me, there were times I needed to be in control in order to settle my mind and feel comfortable in my own skin. If this was going to work between us, he'd need to be okay with that.

By the time we got out of the shower, I was feeling damn good, floating in a happy place on all the endorphins Bomber had stirred up in me. As we dried off, we continued to share kisses and touches like we were teenagers unable to get enough of each other.

When we headed into the bedroom, I realized that while I'd bared my soul to him, Bomber hadn't told me about his upbringing.

"Where did you grow up? I don't know anything about your past, and now you know more about me than anyone else in the club." Well, apparently Keys knew too, but since I hadn't actually told him, that didn't count.

He shrugged a shoulder before he leaned down to gather his clothes from the floor. "Not much to tell. Raised on a ranch out of town. There wasn't any spare money around for me to go off to college, so I figured the military was a good bet. My grandfather had been in the Air Force, so it made sense to follow his lead. I was an only child, so no siblings. It's all pretty boring, really."

I was sure his life hadn't been nearly that simple, and I found I wanted to know more.

"What'd you do for fun when you were growing up?"

He grinned at me. "I wasn't a troublemaker, if that's what you're asking. We were far enough out of town that I didn't have a bunch of friends to hang out with outside of school. I'd always had an affinity with animals, so I'd take in injured or orphaned wildlife and rehabilitated them until they could be released back into the wild."

That reminded me of something. "What happened to the baby skunk?"

He smirked again. "I took it in, of course. Double Trouble are helping take care of her as part of their punishment for pulling the kits out of their nest in the first place. Although, they're both loving it, so not sure it's exactly gonna stop them from doing it again."

"So, it's at Scout's place? Needles?"

"Nah, it's at mine. I've got her set up out on the back porch in a hutch. The girls are coming over to feed it and clean out the cage while I've been away."

I got back to dressing. "So you'll release her once she's big enough?"

"I was thinking I might keep her actually. She's a sweet little thing, and her momma did spray the bitch but good."

I shook my head with a chuckle. Now I wasn't in the middle

of dealing with Karen, in the aftermath, I could see the funny side.

"Yeah, but what happens when she grows up and sprays *you*?"

I grabbed my boots and socks then sat on the edge of the bed to pull my socks on.

"I'll take her in to get her scent glands removed soon, then she'll be harmless as a kitten."

I shook my head. A pet skunk. Fucking nuts.

By the time we headed downstairs, I was feeling torn and I stalled out halfway through the main room. Part of me wanted to man up and go deal with Karen. She was my mess to clean up, but a bigger part of me never wanted to even see the woman again, let alone talk to her.

Bomber's hand landed on my shoulder. "Let the club deal with her, Bank. You don't have to ever see that bitch again. You know she'll only spew more bile your way, on top of all that bullshit she's been feeding you." His palm tightened a moment before he released me. "Go grab a drink and take a seat, let me go see what's going on. You've spoken to your boss? When do you need to return to work?"

I winced, having forgotten all about my job. "Fuck. I was supposed to go back yesterday. Dammit. I'll give my boss a call."

Although, with how he'd been about me taking the time off in the first place, I was pretty sure I was now unemployed. Not like the club owned a landscaping business that I could work at, so it looked like I'd be in for a career change real soon.

As Bomber headed toward the back stairwell, I pulled my phone out and hit dial, figuring I might as well get this call over with.

Bomber

Before I went downstairs to see who was in with Karen, I headed down the hall toward Scout's office. I knocked on the door frame before I entered the open doorway.

"Hey, Prez."

He leaned back from his desk, running his gaze over me as he grinned.

"Bomber. You and Bank get in all right last night?"

I rolled my eyes, "Fucking perv. You know full well we did. I ain't giving you details, but yeah, my boy's back home and in one piece. I do need to talk to you about something to do with him, though."

"Karen's down in lock-up. She's had a very uncomfortable night with bright lights and loud music. Waiting on you and Bank before we tried to question her this morning."

It was good to hear she was already being tormented, but that wasn't what I wanted to discuss. "This isn't about Karen. I left Bank out in the main room to call his boss, but I get the feeling he's about to be fired."

Scout slammed his fist on the desk with a curse, "Never did like that fucker he works for. What were you thinking?"

"Bank does solid work, right? He's experienced enough to take on some prospects to train up. Why not have the club start a landscaping business?"

Scout leaned back in his chair again as he ran his hand through his hair. He used to always wear a bandana that he'd adjust about a hundred times a day, but I hadn't seen it since I'd been back.

"It's not a bad idea. We're running out of places to put the new prospects, and we're getting more and more men interested in joining us. Only so much work at the bike shop, and Athena is only going to be an option for a select few who have the right skills. I can't see any prospects lining up to take shifts at the daycare center." He chuckled. "Although, changing diapers could become a new form of punishment for them if they piss us off. And there's only so much guard duty work we have. Chat with Bank about it, get him to draw up what he'd need and bring it to church on Saturday. I'm sure it'll get voted through."

Blade strode into the office. "We ready to go see what Karen has to say for herself?"

Scout stood, closing the lid on his laptop. "Let's get this over with. You coming, Bomber? Is Bank?"

"I'm in, but Bank's sitting it out. I don't want her to have a chance to crawl in his head again. She's done enough damage."

Scout frowned my way. "Can you confirm she was doing more than fucking with his head?"

I nodded. "Yeah, man is covered in bruises, cuts and scars. And he's real worried the club is gonna boot him out for either Karen's drug dealing or for being with a man. She's done a number on him mind, body and soul."

"They were together for three years. Plenty of time for her to get in his head. Fuck. I've never liked hurting a woman, but I can't wait to mess this bitch up."

I gave Scout a nod, feeling the same way.

"One thing the mob teaches its men well is how to torture an enemy. I'm more than ready to put my skills to good use on her."

Blade was another new face that appeared while I'd been gone. He'd been sold to the mob in L.A. by his father as a boy and risen through the ranks, but he'd always hated the life and broke free with some help from Mac. Now he was here living club life with his old lady.

I followed the other two down to the back of the clubhouse, avoiding the main room so Bank wouldn't see us and try to join in. We were nearly at the bottom of the stairs when loud music started up. Some sort of fucked-up heavy metal garbage I'd never voluntarily listen to.

"What is this shit?"

Blade clapped my shoulder. "Mind games, my brother. Getting her nice and softened up for the physical torture portion of the festivities.."

Scout growled beside me. "Cut that shit out. *We* don't need to be fucking tortured."

Blade moved down to a bunch of controls beside a door and flipped a couple switches that brought blissful silence.

"Thank fuck for that."

I rubbed my ears as Scout unbolted the door and pulled it open. The sight it revealed had me grinning. Karen was tied to a metal chair that was bolted to the floor. Still wearing the dark jeans and tight black tee-shirt she'd had on when I'd caught her the previous day, she also still had dirt smudges on her arms and face from my takedown. Her blonde hair was a ratty, tangled mess, and her eyes were red from either crying or sleep deprivation. Suddenly, half a dozen extra lights came on and I automatically raised my palm to shield my eyes from the brightness.

Scout bellowed out the doorway, "Blade! For fuck's sake, turn all that shit off while we're in here, dammit."

"Sorry, Prez, they're on timers. Turning them off now."

I looked at Scout. "Brother is inventive."

He nodded. "That, he is, but damn, that shit was bright. Fuck.

Okay, let's do this." As Blade came in and closed the door behind him, Scout marched over to the chair and with a fist full of her hair, yanked her head back.

"Who you running drugs for, Karen?"

She laughed, the sound rough as her throat was no doubt dry. "I ain't telling you shit. You think a little music and light therapy is gonna make me chatty, you got another think coming."

With that, Scout pulled out his knife and cut off the zip ties holding her down before he grabbed her arm in a bruising hold and pulled her to stand.

"Let's go next door then, see how fast you start talking once we get some blood flowing."

She stumbled but none of us moved to help her as Scout dragged her toward the door that Blade opened for him. I followed after them, rage building with every step.

"You don't hurt women. No one in this pansy-ass club would ever lift a hand to a lady."

Scout thrust her into the torture room, and she fell to her hands and knees. I walked straight up to her and delivered a swift kick to her gut, flipping her over with the momentum. Grabbing her other arm, making sure I held tight enough to leave a bruise, I lifted her up and tossed her into the chair before I spat the words into her face.

"Pity you ain't a lady then, huh?"

Before she could recover from my winding her, Blade had her ankles strapped down and Scout had handled her wrists. This chair was like a fucked-up dentist chair that would make it possible for all sorts of fun shit. I held her gaze while she was tied down. The fear in them had me feeling a little calmer, but it wouldn't save her. Not after what she'd done to my boy.

Scout nudged me and I shifted back to let him take center

stage.

"Wanna talk yet?"

Her eyes bounced around the room. The wall of implements, the table, the buckets... This room was clearly set up for one purpose and she was locked in tight right in the center of it.

"You wouldn't really hurt me, I'm Bank's old lady."

The club president shook his head. "He never patched you, darlin'. He never came to the club and declared that you were under his protection as his old lady and thank fuck for that, because I wouldn't have ever wanted to take a fucking bullet for you." Without taking his eyes off her face, he called out to us, "She's looking a little dehydrated, brothers. How about we fix that."

With a flick of a lever, Scout lowered the back of the chair. Blade grabbed a bucket of water, and I snatched up a cloth. Looked like a little old-fashioned waterboarding was where we were starting shit off.

Chapter 12

Bank

I was on my third whiskey, trying to drown out the fact I was now unemployed when Scout came storming in from the back with his phone to his ear. "All brothers not guarding the women need to be at the clubhouse right fucking now. Tell Tiny to grab his woman and bring her in, pronto. She's on lockdown until we get this shit sorted."

He hung up and looked my way with fire in his eyes. What the fuck had Karen told them? I downed the rest of my drink before I stood with only a little wobble and moved his way.

"What the fuck did she do?"

He raised a brow at me. "Go get a fucking coffee and go into church. I need you sober, Bank. I need every fucking brother on alert and ready to go."

I turned toward the kitchen a little too quickly and had to put my hand out to the wall. Before I stumbled one more step, Bomber was there, wrapping his arm around my waist from behind and guiding me down the hallway.

"I take it your boss fired you?"

"Yeah. Fucker. Never liked me 'cause of the club. Think he's been looking for an excuse to cut me loose for a while."

"I had a chat with Scout earlier. Might have a solution for

you, but first we gotta deal with Karen's shit."

Once in the kitchen, he all but lifted me onto a chair before he went over to the row of pod machines and got one going. I hoped it was a fucking espresso because I'd not eaten all day then slammed all that whiskey, so I was fucked.

While the coffee did its thing, Bomber went over to the fridge and started shifting stuff around. I leaned my head down on my arms and closed my eyes, beating myself up for being so weak about being fucking fired that I'd gotten drunk and was now useless to my club. They really would kick my ass out if I kept this shit up.

"Bank, sit up and eat this."

I dragged myself up and as soon as I did, a sandwich on a plate was slid in front of me. Too busy mentally beating myself up, I didn't think, just picked the thing up and started chewing. Then the smell of freshly brewed coffee hit me, and I reached for the mug before Bomber could set it down.

He stayed silent until I'd finished eating and drinking, at which point he switched out my mug for a fresh one.

"We need to get into church. The others should be here by now."

With a nod, I got up, feeling a little steadier on my feet already and headed back to the front of the clubhouse. Bomber stayed close, even sitting beside me once we made it inside church.

A couple minutes later, Scout stood at the front, slammed the gavel then glared till everyone was silent.

"Most of you have no doubt heard that Karen pulled some shit and got Bank locked up. Bomber went up and got him free and he's back safe." He gave me a nod. "Karen was in the wind until yesterday. We started questioning her this morning and it ain't fucking good. The stupid bitch wasn't dealing drugs, she was fucking transporting them for the Soto Cartel."

A chill ran down my spine and I set my mug down onto the floor under my chair, so I didn't drop the damn thing.

"She was working with a Mexican cartel?"

How the fuck had I not noticed that?

Scout nodded. "Not just any cartel, either. Tiny's old lady is Mercedes Soto. Her mother fled Mexico with her when she was just a toddler, so she has no memories of what made her mom flee the country. She's never had anything to do with her father, but I got a bad fucking feeling about this. Keys has noted an increase in Mexican males hanging around Marie's Cafe this past week and now we have this connection, we need to be on high alert. Tiny should be arriving with his woman at any moment, and we'll keep her safe here at the clubhouse until we sort this shit out."

Before he could say more, a commotion outside the room was loud enough to reach through the thick door.

"What the fuck? Bomber, go see what that shit is about."

With a nod, Bomber got to the door and just as he opened it, Tiny yelled out, "Got some Mexican scum that was trying to snatch my woman from Marie's. Whatcha want me to do with him?"

Scout turned to Taz. "Take him down to Blade. See what you can find out. And tell Tiny to get in here. Gypsy is on bar duty, he'll make sure Mercedes stays safe."

Seriously, who needed a damn coffee to sober up when you had all this shit rolling in?

Tiny came storming into the room. A huge bear of a man who loved his woman more than anything else, he was clearly furious that his lady was in danger and ready to do some damage.

"Tell me you didn't kill him."

Scout sounded more than a little tense.

Tiny scoffed as he moved to the front of the room. "Like I'd let someone who threatened my woman off that easy. There's plenty of life left in him for Blade and Taz to play with. Do you know why he came for Mercedes?"

Scout frowned at the big enforcer. "We only just found out the connection. Karen was running drugs for the Soto Cartel. The moment she told us, I started making calls to make sure Mercedes was secured. You know I'd never risk any of our old ladies or kids."

"This is Mercedes family coming for her? Why now?"

Scout shrugged. "No fucking clue, brother. Hopefully the guy you brought in will have some answers for us."

Tiny nodded. "Right. Well, let's get down there and question this bastard."

"Soon, brother. First, I need you to chat with your woman. Ask her what she can remember about her old man. Anything her mother might have mentioned. Get me any information you can. I know how young she was and that it won't be much, but it could be the piece of the puzzle we need for all this shit to make sense."

"Yeah, okay. I'm gonna take her up to our room to do it. I'll let you know if she can think of anything."

With that, he turned and left, not waiting for Scout to end church.

"Well, that's about it for now. Keep your eyes open and if you see any more cartel fuckers around town, call it in and we'll send a crew to grab them."

He hit the gavel, and everyone started to leave but I stayed put for a minute. Bomber's palm landed on the back of my neck.

"You doing okay?"

I shook my head. "I brought trouble down on Tiny and Mercedes by being with Karen. I never even really loved her, just the idea of her. I was so fucking lonely and desperate to be normal." I shook my head. "I've brought all this shit down on everyone's heads."

I stood in a rush, storming out the door and grabbing my phone and keys on my way past the lockers before I headed straight out the door and to my bike. I needed to get away and clear my head.

Bomber

I went to chase after my boy when Scout grabbed my arm.

"Leave him be for now. I've already texted Keg, who was out patrolling, and he'll tail him."

"I don't like leaving him alone when he's hurting, Prez."

He nodded. "I get it, I truly do. But you're gonna have to give him space to blow off steam every now and then. If you crowd him, he'll aim that shit at you, and it won't end well. Let him have his ride. You got some food and coffee into him, so he's fine. He hadn't really drunk that much earlier, he just shot it back too fucking fast on an empty stomach, so it hit him hard."

I got what Scout was saying, but I still didn't like it.

"What the fuck am I supposed to do while he's out there?"

"Well, brother, take your pick. Either go mess up the bitch that started all this bullshit or take a turn with the cartel fucker. We got options for you today."

I laughed at the way Scout made it sound like I had a menu to choose from.

"You're a crazy bastard. You know that, right?"

He slapped me on the back as he headed out of the room. "Gotta be to keep all you fuckers in line."

Couldn't argue with the man on that one. I followed him out and toward the rear of the building, where we once more went down to the basement. Messing with Karen held no appeal. We'd broken her completely earlier, so she'd told us everything she had to give. Now she was nothing but a sniveling mess I didn't want to have to deal with, but this cartel fucker had new information we needed. That, I wanted to hear.

Karen had been shifted back to her original cell. I guess Blade wasn't done fucking with her head, because I could see the light leaking out around the door, which would only happen if all those extra bulbs were on. Thankfully, Scout had told him to hold off on the music bullshit until we were done down here. So, the newest captive was now in the interrogation cell, strapped down and cursing up a storm as Taz waited for us to join in the festivities.

"So far, the man's not sayin' a whole lot that doesn't involve cursing us. I don't know much Spanish, but I know when a man is cussing me out."

Knowing I was the best with Spanish out of those of us in the room, I moved in closer.

"Porqué estabas persiguiendo a la chica?"

"Why were you after the girl?"

He spat at me, but I was far enough away he missed. I turned to Taz. "Get started on him."

He nodded. "Fingernails are always a fun place to start."

Since I was taking on the role of good cop, I stood back with Scout as Taz went to work and started yanking out his nails.

"Cualquier momento que quieras empezar a hablar te voy a detener."

"Any time you want to start talking, this stops."

Jaw clenched, he held my gaze stoically through one whole hand, but when Taz moved to start on the other side, a whimper slipped free. Man was good, though. He didn't break easy.

When Taz ran out of fingers, Scout shook his head with a growl and moved forward. Taz shifted to stand with me as Scout picked up a ballpeen hammer.

"Fuck this slow build up shit. Let's jump to some real pain. And I know you understand English, you son of a bitch."

Without pause, he marched up to the chair and swung the hammer down on the man's right kneecap, making him howl and buck for a few minutes.

"Fucking tell me why you were making a grab for Mercedes or I'll do your other knee. Then I'm gonna get the battery out and hook that up to your fucking balls if I have to. So, stop wasting all our time and fucking tell me what I want to know."

The man was panting now, tears streaming down his face, and he started talking. Fucker even managed to start off in English, but that didn't last long.

"The boss… His wife ran away with his daughter. No trace. Then, when he sent men here to look for the puta a recuperar su dinero, la vimos. Mercedes se parece a su mamá. Tiene que ser ella. Cuando le dijimos al jefe, quería que se la regrese. Ella no sería lastimada. Nunca lastimaría a su hija."

Scout looked to me, and I translated, "Says Mercedes looks like her momma so they knew who she was. His boss wants her brought to him. Apparently, he would never hurt her," I finished with a scoff. Sure, he'd never fucking hurt her. Clearly, Scout had the same thought as with a growl, he brought the hammer down on his right hand, shattering bones.

"Don't fucking lie to me. You don't snatch a woman off the

street if you intend on being fucking nice to her. What does your boss want with her?"

It took a few minutes for him to stop panting enough he could speak again.

"Hay un cartel más grande. El nuevo jefe es joven, buscando una esposa."

I translated again. "Her father wants to marry her off to a rival cartel boss. Guessing he wants to get in good with this other cartel, Prez."

Scout nearly vibrated with his rage. "Mercedes already has a fucking man."

With a wince, like he knew we wouldn't like his answer, the man shook his head, "Not married. Doesn't count."

Scout turned to Taz. "Go tell Tiny he needs to marry that woman ASAP. They can fly to Vegas today and get it done." He turned back to the man as Taz rushed from the room. "Will it get her father off her case if she's married?"

He shrugged a shoulder, as much as he could. "Dudo. El señor Soto quiere recuperar a su hija, quiere saber dónde está su esposa. Él parecia débil cuando se fueron. Él quiere dar un ejemplo."

Fuck. This situation was gonna go south fast. "He doesn't think Mr. Soto will back down. His wife leaving like she did made him look weak and he's out to make an example out of them."

Scout's chin lowered and he glared hard at the man. "Well, he fucked with the wrong woman. Mercedes is under the protection of the Charon MC, and we do not take kindly to anyone messing with what is ours."

With that, he tossed the hammer back on the table and strode out of the room. I followed behind, closing the door as I passed through.

Chapter 13

Bank

The sun was sitting much lower by the time I rolled back into the club lot. As much as the ride helped calm me, the moment I saw the clubhouse, I tensed again. Karen was still inside those walls. Mercedes was now locked down in there too.

All my fault.

Before I made it to the door, it swung open and Bomber was there, his gaze intense as I approached. He didn't move when I came up to him, and I winced at the hurt flashing in his eyes. Another thing I fucked up.

I opened my mouth to say something, to tell him it wasn't him I was running from, but no words would come out. I had no clue what to say. Then it didn't matter, because he took a fistful of my shirt and pulled me until I crashed into him. His lips slammed over mine, and everything in my world righted as our tongues danced and his strong arms banded around me to hold me against his solid body.

In only a matter of days, this man had become my anchor.

"Get a fucking room, you two!"

Taz's voice held a whole lot of humor and I pulled from the kiss, my cheeks on fire to look past Bomber to see we'd become the focal point of the entire room, which was filling up as it usually did on a Friday night.

Scout called out loud enough for everyone to hear, "So, if you didn't know, Bomber finally got Bank to say yes. Only took him what, six or so years?"

Bulldog, who was sitting next to Scout, thumped his bicep. "Beats the twenty-five it took you to man up for Marie."

That had everyone laughing and thankfully shifting the focus off me and Bomber.

He leaned in to whisper in my ear, "Don't like you taking off like that. You let me come with you next time, yeah?"

I nodded. "Yeah."

I'd felt like something was missing the entire ride and now I wondered if it was the fact Bomber hadn't been there. It was crazy how quickly he was becoming vital to me.

Bomber led me over to sit with Scout, Bulldog, Mac and Taz. The old ladies hadn't arrived yet.

"Where's Tiny?"

I wanted to apologize to the man for bringing this shit down on his woman.

Scout ran his hand through his hair. "He took Mercedes to Vegas. He needs to marry that girl as fast as he can."

I frowned. "Why? He patched her years ago. Why the sudden need for a ring?"

Taz spoke up. "Because our cartel friend downstairs has a tale to tell. Apparently, Mercedes' father wants his little girl back so he can marry her off to a rival cartel to make peace."

I didn't know much about the cartels, but I doubted Tiny marrying Mercedes would be a quick fix. "And he'll just roll over if she's already married? Not sure I believe it would be that simple."

Scout tilted his glass my way. "Smart man. No, it won't be that simple, but it'll make it harder. He can't marry off a woman who's already married. The concerning thing is the fucker saying her old man wants to make an example out of her and her mother for the way her mother ran off. Guess he hasn't worked out she's dead yet. Not sure how that'll go over. We need a game plan, then I'll give him a call. Keys has stripped a heap of information off his phone and is going through it all."

Thoughts ran through my mind. "Karen's still breathing, yeah?"

Scout nodded slowly, frowning my way. "Yeah, why?"

"At a guess, Jorge Soto is also after someone to blame for the bust at the drug exchange. I have no idea if Karen was the one who tipped off the cops, but I doubt he'll care if we can prove it. Maybe if we offer up Karen to them to make an example out of, they'll leave Mercedes alone."

Taz nodded. "Saves us having to deal with her disappearance too. Already gonna have the cartel fucker's body to dispose of. Ol' Ted's only got so much manure."

Because that was how we got rid of bodies. We buried them under a massive pile of cow shit for a month and presto, no more body.

Scout nodded. "I like it. Mac, you agree?"

Mac was the club VP. "Yep, sounds like a plan to me. Let me go run it past Arrow, Keys and Nitro. We can tell the rest of the club tomorrow at church, but I don't think we should wait to get the ball rolling."

He stood to go find the other club officers, and Bomber wrapped an arm around my shoulders before he leaned back on the couch we'd sat on, taking me with him. I held myself rigid for a few moments before I realized no one was going to say anything, then I snuggled in a little until I was comfortable. When Bomber turned to press a kiss to my temple, I barely held in my sigh.

It felt damn good to be able to simply relax and be still. Unlike with Karen, I didn't have to constantly worry about Bomber reacting to shit. Hell, I'd taken off and left the man behind and he'd just glared, told me not to do it again and that was that. All over.

I could get used to this.

With the cartel hanging around town, Scout had decided a family barbecue was a good way to get everyone into the clubhouse where they were safe while he went to call Jorge Soto with our offer. Within half hour of him putting out the call, the clubhouse and rear yard was packed with brothers, their old ladies and all the kids running around. Bomber had gone to his place and returned with the little skunk that Ash and Ariel were doting over and carrying around like it was a damn baby.

Bomber and I were back in the main room when a commotion at the front door silenced the place.

Jazz came in first. "Mac! Come deal with your damn daughter."

Sparrow came in next, a little roughed up but her chin was up and there was fire in her gaze. A glance at her knuckles confirmed she'd been in a fight, but when Keg came in next, with a familiar teen in his arms, my heart fell through the floor.

Bomber

There was never a dull moment around the clubhouse, especially now we had a bunch of kids and teens around.

Sparrow was a spitfire of a kid. The club had rescued her

from a mob-run brothel in L.A. last year, but instead of going with the rest of the victims to the authorities, she'd stowed away in the club's van and hitched a ride home. Mac and Zara had taken her in, and she was settling in well. At least I thought she had, but by the looks of things, she'd gotten into one helluva fight tonight.

"Neveah!"

Bank's voice was raw, and I was a step behind my boy when he took off toward Keg, who was holding a battered teen in his arms.

Mac came running into the room to join the chaos. "Sparrow, what the hell?"

"Yell all you want. I wasn't gonna let them finish her off. And if it happened again, I'd do the same damn thing."

Jazz rubbed his hands over his face. We'd all seen the sparks that flew between him and Sparrow, but she was way too young for Jazz to be claiming her, so he mostly kept his distance.

Bank carefully took the girl from Keg, so focused on her that he didn't hear the man's question.

"You know her?"

I answered for him, loud enough for everyone in earshot to hear. "She's his sister. They haven't seen each other in years."

Veronica came over and laid a hand on Bank's arm. "Take her up to your room, I'll grab my bag and be right up. Unless you want to take her to the hospital?"

Bank looked shattered and clearly, he wasn't going to be able to answer much while he was still trying to process what had just gone down. Neveah was clinging to her brother and had buried her face in against his neck. She wasn't going anywhere without him.

I turned to Sparrow. "What happened to her? We need to

know if she needs the hospital."

"I was walking over here when I came across this group of guys. Three were younger, around my age, and one was older. The younger ones were holding a girl who was trying to get free, then the older one grabbed her and threw her to the ground. When they all started kicking her, I had to help her. Then Jazz turned up, then Keg, and here we are." She frowned over at Neveah. "I don't know if she needs the hospital, she just shook her head when we offered earlier."

I looked to Veronica. "Head upstairs with them and let us know if you think she needs to be transported. Hopefully there's nothing broken. I'll be up in a few minutes."

Once Veronica led Bank out of view, I turned my focus to Mac. "Can we have your office to get the full story out of these three in private?"

He nodded and we all followed him down to his office, away from the rest of the club. This was going to cause enough of a stir without all the particulars being aired in the main room.

As soon as the door shut, Mac turned on the other men. "Jazz, what's your version?"

"When Scout put the call out that families needed protecting, I started following Sparrow. I know she walks around town a lot and wanted to make sure she was safe. When I saw those fuckers had a girl, I rushed to get to her because I knew she'd dive in the middle of it. As I was running down the street, I sent a text to Keg to bring a cage. By the time he arrived, I'd knocked out one of the little bastards, and the others ran for a car that was parked on the road and took off."

Sparrow bristled, shoving Jazz. "Hey, *I* took that one out. Well, I at least weakened him for you."

He gave her a raised eyebrow. "Sure, babe. You totally had it handled and I just came in and cleaned up the stragglers."

Mac growled and they both silenced. "What did the girl say to you afterward?"

Sparrow shrugged. "Not much. She mumbled some, but I couldn't understand her. I asked if she wanted the hospital, and she shook her head and got a panicked look in her eyes. Then Keg pulled up with a car and here we are."

Mac looked to me. "What do you know about her?"

I needed to tread carefully with this answer, since I knew Bank wouldn't want the whole club knowing his history. "They're half siblings, different fathers. He hasn't seen her since his grandparents passed years ago."

When I didn't say more, Mac nodded, no doubt drawing the right conclusions before turning his attention back to Jazz. "What'd you do with the kid you knocked out?"

"Left him where he lay. Once the others got a look at my cut, they knew they'd fucked up and didn't put up much of a fight before they took off. I snapped some photos of him, and I've got the license plate number to pass on to Keys so he can keep an eye out for them on the cameras around town."

Mac nodded. "Good thinking. Email them through to him now along with the address where you found them. Everyone get going, except for you, Sparrow. We got more to discuss, young lady."

I led the way back to the main room but didn't hang around. I took the stairs two at a time, then rushed down the hallway toward Bank's room.

Chapter 14

Bank

Veronica hurried ahead of me and since we'd left the door unlocked earlier, she wasted no time in opening it for us. Before I made it more than a of couple steps into the room, she'd already rushed to the bathroom and returned with a clean towel.

"Let me lay this on the bed before you set her down."

Veronica didn't bother pulling the comforter off first, just laid the towel over the top and I leaned over to deposit Neveah, but she clung to my neck.

"It's okay, Nee, I'm not leaving you, I promise. Let me put you down so we can check where you're hurt."

Stiffly, she released her grip on me, and I forced myself to rise but stayed right by the bed as Blade came in with a large bowl of steaming water and a backpack.

"Got your kit, little dove. And some warm, soapy water to clean her up in case she's not up for a shower." He turned his attention to me. "I can go check with Sparrow to see if she's got a change of clothes lying around here for her, if you want?"

I ran my gaze down Neveah's body, taking in the muck and dirt on her shirt and jeans, the grime on her hands and face, before I looked up to Blade. "I'll get her in the shower after we're done. If you could check with Sparrow that'd be great."

I moved away to grab the bowl from Blade and winced as she grabbed for my leg. "Not leaving the room, Nee. Promise."

What the fuck had she been through before those punk ass kids got hold of her?

Placing the bowl on the nightstand, I wrung out the washcloth floating in it before I leaned over and wiped at her face, taking most of the blood and dirt off.

Once Veronica set her bag aside and Blade had left the room, she sat on the mattress to look Neveah in the eye.

"Sweetie, I know this must all be really scary, and you probably just want to be alone with your brother, but we need to make sure you don't have any serious injuries first, okay? I'm a Registered Nurse and I work at the hospital here in Bridgewater, so I know what I'm doing. Can you tell me what happened? How you were hurt."

The way her eyes bounced between Veronica and me broke my heart. "Ain't nothing you can say that'll have me abandoning you, Nee. Not ever."

She frowned, tears filling her eyes. "Why'd you block my calls then?"

I shook my head. "I didn't know your number to block."

"I called about a month ago and a woman answered. She said you were busy but when I tried later, the call wouldn't go through."

I squeezed my eyes shut. Was there anything Karen didn't fuck up?

"Dammit! I'm sorry, Nee. That was my ex. She must have blocked your number on my phone. I didn't know you'd rung. What's been going on?"

She looked toward Veronica. "Nothing's broken, I just got beat up some." Then she turned back to me. "I had nowhere else to go, so I hitched a ride over here in the hope I could find you. It was such a dumb idea. When the guy who picked me up was already heading here, I thought I'd hit the jackpot. But when we got into town, he started telling me I needed to think about how I could pay for my ride." She shuddered. "He wanted me to blow him, then let him fuck me. When I refused, he got really angry and was driving too fast for me to try to get out. He didn't stop until he pulled up beside a bunch of boys. I jumped out and tried to run but they grabbed me. Then he got out and came over to me."

She crossed her arms over her chest, rubbing her palms over her biceps. Tears ran down her face as I dropped to my knees beside her and pressed my forehead against hers. I wanted to know what sent her running in the first place, but we needed to deal with any injuries she had first.

"I tried to get away, Justin. I did. But there were too many of them. They had my arms pinned when I managed to kick the guy that had given me the ride in the nuts. That's when they threw me to the ground and started kicking me. Then that girl came in and tried to stop them and you know the rest."

Veronica gently laid a hand on her leg. "You did good trying to fight them off, honey. I'll leave you with your brother but if after your shower you want me to check anything, have him call for me, okay?"

She nodded then Veronica was gone, but she left her bag behind. Guess she figured I could slap on a few Band Aids if she needed them.

Before the door could close, Bomber slipped inside but stayed back from the bed. I turned back to Neveah.

"What sent you running in the first place, Nee?"

With a sigh she closed her eyes. "Mom's crazy. Like she should be in a padded cell, kinda crazy. Dad ran off about six months ago and Mom decided she'd self-medicate with her own choice of drugs and drink. She ain't working, so there's no money, and her dealer thought I was real pretty." She opened her lids to look me in the eye. "And she didn't even try to stop him, Justin! I was closer to the door than him, so I turned and ran. Didn't look back."

I slumped lower down. "You don't blame me?"

She frowned at me then flicked her gaze over my shoulder to where I knew Bomber was moving closer.

"Blame you for what? Yeah, I got really mad that your phone wasn't working when I needed you. But I'd hoped you might have just changed your number or something. That if I could find you, you'd help me."

"The rape is what fucked up her head, it's my fault—"

She shook her head in sharp movements as fire lit her eyes.

"That's utter bullshit and you should know it. Yeah, the rape screwed with her head, but only because Grandma wouldn't allow her to go get the counseling she should have gotten. Prayer doesn't fix everything! You didn't ask to be born into the situation you were. You were an innocent baby that she laid all sorts of blame on."

Bomber's warm palm wrapped around the back of my neck, soothing me as tears leaked down my cheeks for all my sweet sister had suffered, and in relief that she wasn't blaming me for causing it.

"Hey, Neveah, my name is David, but everyone around here calls me Bomber. I'm your brother's boyfriend. He's told me all about you, and well, I wish it was under better circumstances, but I'm happy to meet you. And sweetheart, you will always be welcome and safe with us."

Bomber

Once Blade delivered a change of clothes he'd gotten from Sparrow, Bank helped his sister into the bathroom. I sat on the edge of the bed waiting for him to come back out.

When he did appear, he looked utterly wrecked and I stood to rush over to him, to wrap him in my arms and draw him in against me.

"We'll take care of her, Bank. She's safe now."

His arms tightened around my waist as he buried his face in against my neck. My poor boy had one helluva day.

"Come sit with me on the bed."

Taking his hand, I led him over and after climbing up onto the mattress, I pulled him down so he laid beside me, him on his back, and me on my side looking down at him.

"I'm guessing you had no idea your mom was so far gone?"

He shook his head. "My grandparents never mentioned her, and they made damn sure I stayed out of sight when she'd drop Neveah off or pick her up. She used to work at a gas station."

Curious at how far his sister had run, I asked, "How far from Bridgewater did they live?"

"About forty minutes east of here, in Winnie."

I winced. "Long damn way for her to hitchhike."

He nodded but kept his gaze on the ceiling. "So much could have gone wrong, and for Sparrow to be the one to come up to them? For her to end up here?" He paused for a minute. "I'm grateful to that girl."

"You were there when the club rescued her, weren't you?"

He nodded again. "Yeah, we went over to L.A. to deal with Sabella when he came after us one too many times. Together with Blade's help, we went in and shut down his whorehouse. Fucker had a room of kids and when we opened that door, Sparrow was front and center, ready to take us all on to keep those other kids safe. She's a fighter."

"Guessing she's gonna be Neveah's new best friend after how they met."

That got a hint of a smile. "Yeah, I can see that happening. They can be Double Trouble, Take 2."

I ran my hand over his stomach, needing to touch him. "They ain't bringing home any more skunks, though. One's enough."

He barked out a laugh, just as I'd hoped he would before he grew serious again.

"What if she comes looking for her? Tomorrow morning, she might have a moment of lucidity and come for her. She'll no doubt work out where I am and then try looking for her here." He turned to lock his pain-filled gaze with mine. "I can't let her go back there."

I leaned down and kissed him soundly on the lips before I pulled back and stroked my hand down the side of his face.

"We won't let anything happen to that girl ever again, and I'll talk to Scout about how they worked the paperwork for Sparrow. If they could make her adoption legal, they can deal with this. You're her brother, for fuck's sake. Mac and Zara were perfect strangers to that girl."

Bank leaned into my touch as I stroked his face. "According to the paperwork, she's Mac's niece or something, but yeah, let's get that shit sorted soon. I want her safe."

"You'd really do that for me?"

Neither of us had heard the door open so I had no clue how long Neveah had been listening. I looked up at the teen, who was still hovering in the doorway, tugging on the borrowed shirt she was wearing.

"You and Bank can live with me at my new place. It's on the same street where Sparrow lives, so she'll be close by if you want to see her again."

She chewed her lip but nodded.

Bank swung his legs over so he sat on the edge of the bed a moment before he stood. I moved over but stayed sitting on the bed as Bank went to her. I knew Bank hadn't wanted to move in with me so soon, but he couldn't live here at the clubhouse with Neveah, and his old house was a mess with the cartel nearly destroying it.

"Is that what you want? To live with me and Bomber here in Bridgewater? I'm sure we can get you transferred to the school here and shit."

Her gaze flicked to me for a moment before it returned to her brother. "Yeah, I'd like that. I can't go home. She really is crazy, Justin."

My boy nodded. "We'll see what we can do about that too. You hungry? I'm sure there's plenty of food downstairs by now. And I can guarantee that Sparrow is still hanging around somewhere."

No doubt with Jazz still stalking around after her too, but I wasn't going to say that out loud.

"Food would be good."

Scooping his sister up into his arms, Bank headed out into the hallway, me on his heels, loving how sweet my boy looked caring for his little sister. A girl I was already feeling damn protective over myself.

Suddenly a thought hit me that left me wincing. Fuck. Guess I was gonna be a girl dad after all. Hopefully, Neveah wouldn't get in as much trouble as Ash and Ariel did. Although,

Sparrow was her age and she still caused her folks enough worry.

Chapter 15

Bank

The next day was a whirlwind of activity. We had to go buy a bed and other shit for Neveah then get it all set up. I'd also grabbed a few things for myself, since the cartel had trashed everything at my old place. It all needed to be done, but it meant I didn't get a chance to call Scout about getting all the paperwork sorted until after she'd gone to bed for the night.

I was on edge, fearing that somehow our mom would figure out where she was and rock up on our doorstep, making demands.

With a sigh, I dropped down into the couch next to Bomber, who slung his arm around my shoulder and drew me in tight against his side.

"I need to call Scout about getting shit sorted."

"You do but kiss me first."

With a smile, I leaned up to press my lips to his. The soft kiss rapidly grew heated and with a growl, Bomber pulled me over his lap so I straddled him, the layers of clothing not doing much to hide either of our hard-ons as we ground together.

With a groan, I pulled back, resting my forehead against his as I squeezed my eyes shut. "We don't have time right now, dammit."

"I know, but later? You're all mine, boy."

I pushed myself back so I could look him in the eye. "You okay with this? I know you wanted me to move in, but now you got an instant family. We've only just started dating. It's all happening so fast, I'd understand if you—"

Bomber didn't let me finish before he had his hand around my throat and was pulling me in for another hot, hard kiss.

"You are exactly where I want you, boy. I already feel protective over Neveah, and I don't have a problem becoming a dad overnight. And while we've only been official for a few days, we started this thing years ago. We're good, Bank. So, give Scout a call and get our girl sorted. Then later, I'll let you know just how okay I am with the recent developments."

I shook my head, thinking this man was too good to be true. "I'm falling hard for you, David."

He cupped my face in both his palms. "Good thing that, because you got my heart in your hands, Justin."

Leaning in, I captured his mouth with mine, sharing another long, slow, drugging kiss before I reluctantly pulled back and shifted off Bomber's lap. Needing to keep contact, I moved to sit against the side arm and after kicking off my boots, laid my legs over Bomber's lap. His palms were running up and down my calves by the time I had my phone out and to my ear.

The phone only rang once before Scout picked up. "Bank, your sister settle in okay?"

"Yeah, Prez. She's tucked in for the night, safe and sound. But I wanna keep her that way. How'd you sort out Sparrow's adoption?"

"We called in a favor from a friend, but I don't think we'll need that for Neveah. While you and Bomber were sorting out her physical needs today, Keys and I, along with some help from Jacie, got a plan in place for tomorrow. I gotta do the hand-off to Jorge Soto tomorrow night, but we have the day to get your shit sorted."

My heart skipped a beat. "Jorge is coming up himself? Are Tiny and Mercedes back yet?"

"They fly in tomorrow morning and Jorge is insisting on meeting Mercedes at the hand-off. It was the one condition he refused to shift on. He is accepting Karen as a trade-off and has promised to leave the club alone in return."

I nodded even though he couldn't see me. "That's good. So long as he doesn't make a play for Mercedes at the meet."

"We'll have Taz and the other snipers set up watching. She'll be safe. Now, as for Neveah, we're going to head over to Winnie and pay your mom a visit. Easiest way to get her into your custody is to have her sign the paperwork. I got a feeling we can be convincing enough to get that done. It'll also mean Neveah can pack up her stuff to bring back with her."

I rubbed a hand across the back of my neck over what I was gonna request next. "Scout, our mom…" I sighed. "There's a good reason she's like she is."

His voice softened. "Keys told me the details, brother. You want to get her help? That's your choice, but we can get her into care at Pieces to Peace if you want."

My gaze found Bomber's and he squeezed my calf as he smiled at me. He was only hearing half the conversation, but he was a smart man. He could guess at what Scout was saying.

"Yeah, that'd be good, Prez. She never had a chance. Her folks—my grandparents—were real religious. Thought prayer could fix everything. She never got the help she needed back when it happened."

"Sadly, not a rare situation, but it's never too late to get help. Once she signs over Neveah's custody to you, we'll get her into care. Get her off the drugs she's got herself on, then onto proper meds that'll actually help her."

My throat clogged with emotion for a moment, and I had to cough to clear it before I could speak. "Thanks, Prez."

"Anytime, brother. You're a Charon, and we all have your back. Speaking of which, you got fired today, didn't you?"

That had me wincing. Another thing I had to worry about. "Yeah. Boss never liked that I was a Charon."

"Yeah, we had some history back in school. Never did like that little fucker. Anyway, what do you think of starting up your own business? Together with the club, I mean. You can take on some of the newer prospects and brothers and train them up."

Shock had me sitting completely still. "Are you serious?"

"Of course, I am. Your man came to me asking about it, and I agree it's a good fucking idea. Get together a business plan, some figures and shit, and present it at church next week. We'll have a vote and get you set up."

When I stayed silent, still too shocked to speak, Scout chuckled.

"Go get some sleep and be ready to ride out at oh-eight hundred. I got a van sorted for Neveah's things so you can take her on your bike with you. And we'll figure out everything else later. We got your back, Bank."

After I managed to mumble a thank you, I hung up and looked to Bomber. Overwhelmed, I wasn't sure what to say. But it didn't matter, my man knew me. He gently moved my legs off his lap so he could stand, then reached a hand down to me. Without hesitation, I took it, and he pulled me up, then led me to his—no, *our*—bedroom. As I followed behind him, my hand in his, I decided I'd tell Neveah about tomorrow's plans later. First, I wanted inside my man.

Bomber

I'd spoken to Scout earlier in the day, so I knew what he was going to offer Bank, and from the half of the conversation I'd heard, I was guessing my boy had taken up the club president on all his suggestions. Which meant tomorrow was going to be a long, emotional, exhausting day. All the more reason to make sure Bank got a good night's sleep tonight.

And I knew just how to make him nod off with a smile.

I stayed silent as we made our way to our bedroom. Neveah had thankfully chosen the bedroom at the other end of the house, so we didn't need to worry too much about keeping quiet. But it wasn't for her that I stayed quiet now, it was to give Bank a few minutes to wrap his head around the fact that the club really did have his back and want him around. Karen had done a great job playing on his insecurities until he'd felt so alone all he had was her.

I couldn't wait to see her face when we handed her over to Soto tomorrow. Her life was about to get a whole lot harder, and it couldn't happen to a more deserving bitch.

Once we passed through into our room, I reached behind Bank to close the door before I pressed him back against the timber. The half-lidded gaze he gave me was enough to have my blood pumping and my cock throbbing.

"My turn to claim you tonight."

Bank's voice was rough with arousal, which added to my own as I reached for his shirt, to strip it off him. His hands were just as busy as mine and within minutes and between kisses, we were both naked and stumbling toward the bed. I let myself fall when the back of my knees hit the mattress and

Bank followed me down, lips crashing together again as our hard cocks rubbed against each other, fueling my arousal even higher.

In the past, I hadn't bottomed often for a lover. I was more comfortable being the top but with Bank it was different. I *wanted* it to be different. A partnership where we shared every role in our lives together. And tonight, that meant I was going to let him top me. Let him claim me before I'd roll him over and return the favor.

Bank swiveled his hips, the slide of his dick against mine enough to have me shuddering with a groan.

"Fuck, Bank. You keep this up, it's gonna be over before we start."

He lowered his face and bit at my collarbone. "I have faith that you'll rally quickly for round two."

That pulled a growl from me, but my boy just laughed, a husky sound that had me gripping his hips and pulling him down tightly against me for a few moments. Then it was Bank shuddering and cursing before he pulled from my grip and slid off the bed. I didn't move as my gaze followed him as he headed to the side closet. My boy was a fine sight from the back, his ass so fuckable, I wanted to take a damn bite out of it. However, I needed to wait my turn tonight. Fucking loved that he wanted to claim me like I had him.

I wrapped my palm around my cock as I continued to watch him grab the lube and condoms. While we had managed to fit in a trip to the doctor's today, the tests weren't back yet. I couldn't wait for the time when we could fuck with nothing between us. With how I was feeling toward Bank, I would have said fuck the tests and gone bareback, but Karen was an unknown risk. We had no clue who she'd been stepping out on Bank with, so it wasn't worth the danger when we just needed to wait another day or so for the all-clear.

Keeping my strokes long and slow, I didn't allow myself to get too close to the edge, not wanting to come until Bank was deep inside me. Ideally, I wouldn't come until I was inside my boy, but I doubted I'd be able to hold off that long.

"You sure you're good with this?"

I nodded. "Haven't bottomed much, so be gentle this first time, but I'm sure I want you to claim me."

With a grin that made him look so damn young, he moved to kneel between my thighs that I'd spread to give him all the room he could need. Still with that grin on his face, he lubed up his fingers on one hand, then shocked the hell out of me when he leaned over to wrap his lips around my cock as his slick fingers slid down over my asshole, rimming the tight muscle as he sucked and licked at my dick.

"Fuck!"

Releasing my hold on my cock, I gripped his head, holding him still as I bucked up into his mouth. I was careful not to go too deep to start with, but by the time he had two fingers pumping into my ass, I was mindlessly fucking his face in time with his movements.

With a growl, I came, filling my boy's mouth. My cock kept kicking out more for him to swallow as he slipped a third finger into my ass, stretching me out.

Loose-limbed from the orgasm, I lay like a rag doll as he slid his fingers free, wiped them on a towel he'd brought over earlier, then sheathed his thick erection with a condom and added more lube.

I kept my gaze on his face as he lined himself up and pressed in. The bliss that flowed over his features as I arched under him, together with the fullness I felt with his dick deep inside me, had my own cock thickening again.

"You feel so fucking good, Justin, but know the moment you finish, I'm rolling you over for my turn."

His whole body shuddered as he thrust in again, stabbing at my prostate and sending a wave of heat through me.

"That sounds perfect."

Yep, this was the perfect way to spend our first night living together. Both of us claiming the other in the most carnal of ways.

When Bank's movements grew jerkier as he closed in on his release, I reached up to grip the front of his neck. I'd noticed how he melted for me whenever I did it, and I fucking loved to feel his pulse under my fingers, knowing that he lived and was healthy.

I used my grip to pull him down so I could bite at his lower lip, tugging it before I growled into his mouth before kissing him hard. It was sloppy and hot and within seconds, he groaned as he came, warmth filling my channel as he emptied himself into the condom.

He went to slide off, but I held my grip until he stilled and looked into my gaze.

"Love you, Justin. You own my fucking heart."

His eyes glazed over with moisture, and he leaned in to press a kiss so gentle, it rocked my damn soul.

"Feeling the same way, David. Don't ever leave me."

Releasing my hold on his throat, I wrapped my arms around him to pull him down against my chest as my own eyes stung a little at the bond I was forming with this man. My heart and soul, who was still scared I'd fucking abandon him.

"Never, Justin. You're stuck with me for life. Especially, now that we have a teenager to raise."

That got me a watery chuckle before he pulled free of my body, tossed the condom then returned so I could have my turn at rocking his world.

Epilogue

Thursday 28ᵗʰ November 2019
Bank

Pulling up out the front of Pieces to Peace, the center the club helped set up last year, I didn't have to wait long for Neveah to come bounding out to me. The grin on her face was only a little strained, so hopefully she'd had a good visit.

I held her custom helmet out to her. "Mom doing good today?"

"Yeah, but I still can't get her to agree to see you."

I pulled her in for a sideways hug. "You need to stop with that one. She's never gonna change her opinion of me, no matter what any of us say or do."

She huffed out a frustrated breath as she pulled from my hug to put her helmet on. "It's so ridiculous. She has to know you and your club are paying for her to stay here. She won't even acknowledge you're her son, but you're the one taking care of her."

I shook my head at my little sister. "Doing the right thing isn't about what we'll get in return for the action. I'm getting better at remembering it isn't my fault she's the way she is, but it isn't her fault, either. Everyone deserves to be loved and cared for. Hopefully, one day, she'll be able to leave this place and have a life free of the chains that she's been bound in for so long."

With a roll of her eyes, she hopped up behind me. "Hate when you make sense. Let's get rolling. Sparrow said it's going to go off tonight."

With a laugh, I gunned the engine and rolled out of the drive. Before I hit the road, movement caught my eye and I turned to catch a glimpse of Mom pulling away from a window. I gave a little wave, unsure if she was still watching then took off toward the clubhouse.

It was Thanksgiving and Sparrow was right, the clubhouse would be rocking. Unfortunately for the teens, it wouldn't really get going until well after they were back home, asleep. Mac and Zara had offered to have Neveah for a sleepover so Bomber and I could have a date night, which was sweet of them, and I couldn't wait to get some alone time with my man.

Neveah whistled when I pulled into the packed lot of the clubhouse, and I chuckled again. This was her first big club party, and she was in for some surprises.

"Everything will be all set up outside."

Taking her hand, I led her through a nearly empty front room and down the hallway toward the rear yard. The moment we passed through the door, the sounds of people having fun surrounded us. The younger kids were running around screaming and laughing, Sparrow was off in a corner doing a very poor job of not watching Jazz, who was with the other younger brothers, doing an equally bad job of not showing off for the girl.

Bomber came over and after giving me a kiss hello, turned to give Neveah a hug. "How was your mom today?"

She hugged him back without hesitation, and I fucking loved how quickly we'd formed a little family. "She's doing okay.

The new meds are helping, and she told me she's started participating in group therapy time now."

"That's great, Nee."

He released her and with a wave, she dashed off toward Sparrow. Bomber wrapped his arm around my shoulders and pulled me in.

"Ready for our teen-free night, boy?"

Closing my eyes, I shuddered. "Mmm. Hell, yes."

Before we could say anything else, Scout hollered that everyone needed to shut the fuck up, and Marie told him off for swearing. Once everyone quit laughing, he climbed up on a picnic table that wasn't covered in food and drinks to look out over the whole yard.

"This club has been through a lot this past year, but we've come through, solid and strong as ever. I'm thankful for each and every one of you. This club is a family, and it needs every single one of its members to be whole. So, none of you forget that, and quit getting yourselves in binds that put your lives at risk, dammit."

Another round of chuckles, and my cheeks heated with embarrassment until Bomber pulled me in for a quick hug.

"Now, we got some formalities to take care of." He scanned the crowd. "Where's Neveah? Bomber, Bank, you two get up here too."

Clinging to Sparrow's hand, Neveah nervously made her way to us, then we all headed to where Scout was climbing down off the table. Mac stood beside him, along with Keys and Nitro, and they were all grinning, so I wasn't too worried, but I was curious about what the fuck they were gonna pull.

"Neveah, this is us formally welcoming you to the family. You are now officially a daughter of the club."

Sparrow snatched the cut off her father as soon as he brought it out from behind his back.

"Hey, Sparrow!"

Predictably, she ignored her father and helped a stunned-silent Neveah into her new cut, complete with a Daughter of the Club patch on the front left side, the small red heart wrapped in barbed wire a clear message to anyone who saw it that knew the Charon MC. She was a cherished part of the club family.

Sparrow ushered Neveah away, gushing over her cut that matched her own but when I went to follow, Scout held his hand up.

"She's not the only one getting a new patch. Brothers, since we figured neither of you wanted to switch out your current cut for an old lady one—" He paused for the round of snickering that came from the club. "We opted to get you both a new patch for your current cuts to signify your relationship status."

My lungs struggled to work as Mac stepped up to Bomber, and Scout moved in front of me. He looked me in the eye before he spoke. "As a club, we wanted both of you to know, we accept your claim on each other and respect you as a couple within the club."

With that, he dumped a heap of super glue on the back of a curved patch and slapped it on the lower part of my cut. When I looked down to see what it said, I grinned. "Property of Bomber" was now part of my cut, loud and proud. I glance to Bomber, and I saw he now wore a "Property of Bank" patch in the same position on his cut.

Scout leaned in and spoke in a whisper only I'd hear. "It's good to see you happy, brother, and I'm sorry we didn't step in earlier to deal with the Karen mess. We should have seen you needed help years ago."

I reached a hand out to grip my president's shoulder as I forced down the emotion that wanted to clog my throat.

"It all happened as it was meant to. How it needed to, in order for us to be where we are now."

He nodded. "Amen to that, brother. A-fuckin'-men."

With a whoop, Bomber pulled me away from Scout and cupping my face, pressed his lips to mine. I gripped his waist tightly as he devoured my mouth until I barely knew my own name.

"Whoa, fellas, keep it PG while the kiddos are still around."

Taz's Aussie drawl had heat flaming across my cheeks as I pulled back from my man to see the club all smiling broadly at me.

Could life get any better than this?

Other Charon MC Books:

Book 1:
Inking Eagle

Eagle & Silk

Book 2:
Fighting Mac

Mac & Zara

Book 3:
Chasing Taz

Taz & Flick

132

Book 4:
Claiming Tiny

Tiny & Mercedes (Missy)

Book 5:
Saving Scout

Scout & Marie

Book 6:
Tripping Nitro

Nitro & Cindy

Book 7:
Scout's Legacy

Scout & Marie

Book 8:

Mac's Destiny

Mac & Zara

Book 9:

Losing Bash

Bash

Book 10:

Finding Needles

Needles & Bess

Book 11:

Forging Blade

Blade & Veronica

Book 12:

Taming Keys

Keys & Donna

Book 13:

Breaking Arrow

Arrow & Tabitha

Book 14:

Taz's Guards

Taz & Flick

Book 15:

Shielding Bank

Bank & Bomber